THE ECHO VECTOR

THE ECHO VECTOR

James Kahn

ST. MARTIN'S PRESS

New York

Design by Claire Counihan

Library of Congress Cataloging-in-Publication Data

Kahn, James.
    The echo vector.

    I. Title.
PS3561.A37E24   1987   813'.54   87-13973
ISBN 0-312-01023-0

10   9   8   7   6   5   4   3   2

For Jerome McGann,
conspirator

See, how on the unsubstantial air
I kick, bleating my private woe,
     as upside down my rolling sight
somersaults, and frantically I try to set my world
upright;
     too late learning why I'm hung here,
whose nostrils bleed, whose life runs out from eye and
ear.

—from "The Slaughter-House,"
ALFRED HAYES, 1944

PROLOGUE

At 3:00:01 on the afternoon of Friday, December 20, 1985, security guard Elmore Gray locked the outer door of the Bay City National Bank so nobody else could come in. There were still a dozen customers waiting in line at the tellers' windows, four tellers, three loan officers, a VP, and a few assistants of various kinds; these Elmore would let out in ones and twos, his hand never leaving the key in the door. But he would let no one else in, for it was closing time, and Elmore knew his job. He'd been a security guard for thirty-two years.

And he'd have died of boredom long ago, except for the game he played, the game of guessing who people were.

The man in the Brooks Brothers suit, walking toward him, for example. Distinguished, fiftyish, knew just what he wanted. Not a regular here. Opening a new account, maybe; visiting fireman, more likely—regional director. Wore an Ivy League tie, maroon with gold shields on it.

Elmore opened the door for Ivy League. The man smiled as he exited, and gave Elmore a half salute. "Army," thought Elmore, locking the door again.

Almost immediately there was a small explosion. Elmore turned, reaching for his gun, then stopped. And smiled.

It was a balloon, a little girl's balloon. It had popped while she was standing in line with her mother. Everyone around them had reacted, and Elmore registered these faces now: startled, amused, sympathetic. The girl's mother was reassuring, promising future balloons.

The longhair behind them was laughing his head off, rings jingling all over his face—three earrings shaped like bells, and a *nose* ring, of all things, a rhinestone stud. Guy had to be stoned.

The macho man in the sleeveless T-shirt, with the dragon tattoo on his arm, standing at the head of the line, looked impatient and annoyed, as if the little girl's accident had delayed him. Looked like a troublemaker; Elmore would keep an eye on him.

The head loan officer, Ms. Vargas, began rummaging through her drawer looking for candy to give the girl.

The man with the dragon tattoo got to a teller's window, moving the girl's mother up to the head of the line.

Another teller said, "Next."

The mother and the little girl didn't go up to the teller, though; they got out of line and walked straight toward Elmore.

He opened the door as they approached him.

The mother looked flustered, but not unamused. "I can't believe I forgot my checkbook," she muttered to the universe.

"Have a good day, now," said Elmore. He didn't think she was a regular either. New account, probably. Housewife.

She was out the door as Ms. Vargas stood, holding a

red sucker, took two steps forward, and paused with an expression of mild confusion.

"She got her business done, Ms. Vargas," said Elmore. "You can catch her next time."

Vargas shrugged, tore the cellophane off the candy, stuck it in her mouth, and went back to her desk.

"You a handsome woman, Vargas," thought Elmore, and tried to imagine who *she* might be when she went home and turned out the lights.

Part I

AULD

CHAPTER 1

Jordan Marks sat parked in his silver BMW until "She Loves You" was over—it was a Golden Oldies Weekend on KRTH—then switched off his Blaupunkt, looked at his Rolex, and got out of the car. Five minutes late. Poor Hoffman was probably just starting to panic that Jordan wouldn't show at all. Well, too bad—early Lennon was more important than late Marks.

Jordan walked across the parking lot, out to the front concourse area. Even as late as the twenty-eighth the depressing signs of Christmas in L.A. were still everywhere apparent: palm trees draped with tinsel that at 8:00 A.M. already shimmered in the heat; a pathetic little fir by the door, its flocking parched and powdered by six days of arid wind.

Jordan caught sight of his image in the glass door as it slid open to admit him: Reeboks, Levi's, a taupe silk shirt tailored by a British mail-order firm based in Hong Kong, attaché in hand; just the right cachet of understated overachievement. And then the door was open, and the image was gone, and Jordan stepped through, past this illusion of himself. "Vive les illusions," he

3

thought. He tended to be philosophical, if not actually cynical, on the occasion of his birthday.

The event wasn't, in fact, for two more days, and Jordan had little, in the event, for which to be cynical. At forty minus two days, he was in the best physical shape he'd been in since high school—he worked out regularly at the Sports Connection, his diet was straight Eat to Win with an occasional weekend Wild Turkey. He felt thirty, looked twenty-eight: smooth, easily tanned skin, high cheeks with a classic aquiline nose, black, loose Jewish afro; and those blue blue Paul Newman eyes. Jordan still ranked with the ladies.

And yet his birthday always brought him to a sort of brown study; it was a time of stock-taking in which he usually found himself short-stocked, no matter what his actual circumstances. And so it was this year.

He walked across the lobby, nodding vaguely at the four registration clerks, two of whom, he knew, had active fantasies about him. He crossed the triage area, which was now vacant, and passed through the double doors to the main emergency room, where he put on his happy face and made ready to start the day.

Jordan was an ER doc.

"Hi, Dr. Marks," said Gloria, innuendo lacing every syllable. Gloria was the ward clerk.

"Morning, Glory," said Jordan. He tried to keep his tone neutral, though it was clear to everyone in the place that the two of them had a thing.

Tracy rounded the corner out of the supply room, nearly colliding with Jordan. Tracy was the EMT—emergency medical technician (that which was called orderly in the days before janitors were maintenance engineers). He was eighteen, hip, flip, scrub-shirted, single earringed, double dimpled. "Hey, dude, you're late."

4

"Had to wait for the Beatles to finish. They were appearing in my car."

"Hey, I saw you slippin' out the back of the On Klub last night," Tracy went on, sly smile in his voice.

"Wasn't me," said Jordan. He held out his hand, palm up, Tracy slapped him five, and Jordan walked on. In point of fact, it *wasn't* Jordan that Tracy had seen—Jordan had been home watching "Miami Vice." But the way Jordan denied the charge allowed Tracy to think it *had* been Jordan, which made Jordan's disavowal doubly cool. The two of them had a conspiracy of cool.

Furthermore, Jordan was known as a storyteller. Not that he commonly lied for advantage, exactly; but he'd sometimes exaggerate a story so well and so often that he came to believe his own improvisations as deeply as the hard copy—and he was a master of improvisations. So for Jordan to *decline* to tell a story now, when Tracy had set it up as straight man . . . well that just made the elliptical tale all the stronger by its omission.

Jordan walked around the front desk, stood behind Gloria, put his briefcase on the floor, his hands on her shoulders, and began giving her a neck rub as he leaned over her to view the log book on the desk. The ER log recorded, in tabular form, every patient who entered. It included time and date of entry, diagnosis, doctor of record, time of discharge, and final disposition. This was Jordan's first stop whenever coming on duty. "Any good cases last night?" he asked.

"Mm—more on the left," Gloria spoke from her throat, pressing up on his hand with her shoulder, like a cat.

He reached his right hand over her to the Diagnosis column in the log, brushing the front of her blouse with his sleeve, causing her to exhale audibly—and ran his

5

finger down the list of last night's emergencies: chest pain, gastroenteritis, chin laceration, appendicitis, viral syndrome, cardiac arrest, mixed drug overdose, otitis media, sprained ankle, cardiac arrest, gunshot wound left hand, epistaxis, constipation, tonsillitis, perirectal abscess, viral syndrome, asthma, low back strain. Busy night. Poor Hoffman would be wiped.

Gloria grabbed Jordan's hand and replaced it on her shoulder. "More on the left doesn't mean less on the right," she purred.

Hoffman came out of the trauma room in a bloody surgical gown, peeling off bloody surgical gloves as he walked. Beyond him, Head Nurse Playter was reprimanding Tracy: "I've told you before, no earrings on duty."

As Tracy fluffed his hair out to cover the offending lobe, he replied, "Don't you think the street people need an advocate down here?"

And she handed him a bedpan, deadpan: "Bed four, advocate this."

Jordan picked up his briefcase and met Hoffman at the sink. They traded weary smiles.

"Man, I was afraid you were a no-show," Hoffman shook his head, lathered his hands with Betadine soap.

"Bad night?"

"A pisser. Two full arrests, down the tubes. Now *this* gomer—Cheremoya—in shock from a huge fuckin' posterior nasal bleed . . ."

"Got it plugged?" The question was not one of mere interest. If Hoffman hadn't stopped the bleeding, Jordan might have to try—and a big posterior bleed was a mother to control, as evidenced by Hoffman's blood-soaked gown.

"No, I had to call ENT," Hoffman admitted. The ear, nose, and throat surgeon.

Cheremoya was pushed out of the trauma room on a gurney—a pale old man, most of his color puddling in his sheets—and wheeled out of the area to his next trial.

"Anyway," Hoffman was drying his hands now, "the guy's on his way to the OR, so you don't have to worry about him." They walked around the corner into the small doctors' office behind the nursing station. It contained: a desk whose surface was not visible beneath an incredible clutter of charts, journals, newspapers, scratch papers, lunch dishes, pill samples, hospital memos, a telephone, and, at one end, a computer terminal; a vintage desk chair on wheels; a two-seat, cigarette-burned, sweat-stained, threadbare sofa; two wall shelves full of mostly out-of-date medical books; and a three-foot Christmas tree adorned with various medical oddments, the topmost among them being a plastic vaginal speculum taped at its fulcrum with a pair of half-inflated latex surgical gloves, supposed to pass for angels' wings—yet the whole ill-inspired apparatus looked not so much like an angel as a demented moose. Still, angels, no less than devils, it may be supposed, have worn stranger faces before and since.

On one wall was a bulletin board tacked with notices about CPR and ACLS classes, blood drives, security problems in the parking lot, the ER Christmas party, someone selling a cherry Mustang, needle-stick procedures, car pool information. On another wall was a large calendar printed by a large drug company, depicting a different endoscopic close-up photo of some segment of the gastronintestinal tract for each month of the year. December was the rectum.

7

"So who *do* I have to worry about?" asked Jordan, tossing his briefcase on the couch, putting on a green surgical scrub shirt.

Hoffman gathered his stuff together. "Let's see, there're three players left—a lady in Four with diarrhea, a screaming kid in Two—I haven't looked at him yet—and an asthmatic in Holding Bed One; I think he's asleep now."

Jordan gave a mock salute. "Dr. Marks, ready to take over, sir."

"Ready to *bend* over, you mean." Hoffman grabbed his coat off the chair. "Anyway, I'm off to Palm Springs. See you next week." He walked out the door without looking back.

"Yeah, if you don't die of pleasure first," Jordan called to him. He draped his stethoscope around the back of his neck, the standard emblem of the young doctor.

"Everybody got to die of something," Hoffman yelled back, and disappeared out the double doors.

Bay Cities was a private hospital, though its emergency room treated anybody who walked or was carried in, regardless of financial status. And since it sat on the cusp of a changing neighborhood, it saw a fairly wide cross section of people in crisis.

Jordan's first patient that morning, for example, was a five-year-old Vietnamese boy with circular burn marks covering his chest. Jordan was veteran enough to know it wasn't child abuse—merely a traditional Southeast Asian remedy, consisting of putting fire-heated nickels or drinking glasses on a patient's skin.

His next patient was a man with tennis elbow who was annoyed to have been kept waiting.

Then the cop came in and cuffed a young *cholo* to the

bed: a fourteen-year-old in an undershirt, peacock tattoos up the inside of his forearms, good for covering his (needle) tracks. The boy had a screwdriver sticking through his left bicep and out the other side.

"How'd this happen?" asked Jordan.

The *cholo*, whose name was Gato, shrugged.

The cop, Diaz, said, "He got it for goofin' on someone else's *placa*. You know, spray paint."

"Don't you guys have anything better to do?" asked Jordan, poking around the protruding screwdriver.

"Don't you?" said Gato.

Jordan's next patient was a PCP overdose. It took Jordan, Tracy, Playter, a hospital security man, and two city cops to hold the guy down, buckle his wrists to the gurney in leather restraints. The guy still managed to bite one officer, spit on everyone else, and then twist upright to the floor, the gurney now strapped to his back. He lumbered out of the ER swinging the bed from side to side on his shoulders, bellowing like Rodan, everyone in careful pursuit.

Next was the detail man. Jordan generally tried to dodge these guys, but this one positioned himself in the office doorway, so there was no circumventing the matter. Detail men were the drug company representatives who tried to sell the latest pharmaceuticals to doctors—sell the idea, that is, the notion that the doctors should prescribe these up-to-the-minute remedies to their patients. It was the *patients*, of course, who would then buy the drugs.

Traditionally, detail men (the older ones, anyway) had simple marketing techniques—they would give the doctors lots of free samples, or tickets to local sporting events, complimentary liquor, gimmicks. Bribes, in other words. Abel Winston—now in Jordan's doorway—

was slightly different, in that what he gave, predominantly, was stories. It was an attribute to which Jordan could relate, for though he ordinarily saw these salesmen as alternately annoying or tragic—say, Lomanesque—he did love a good story. So he sat back and allowed Abel "How soon do you want it? I'm able!" Winston his three minutes of spiel.

"Okay, what you got today, Abel?"

"We got the very latest in tranqs," he beamed, opening his briefcase full of brochures, "Your patients'll call you Dr. Svengali. Then we got a new antispasmodic for bypass patients . . ."

"G-I?" Jordan queried.

"G, I don't know," Abel winked. "Reminds me of a story, though. Guy's doctor tells him he's got a tapeworm—very dangerous—they gotta get rid of it. Sure, how? says the guy. Doctor says pull down your pants and bend over. So the guy does, and the doctor shoves a hard-boiled egg up there, counts to fifty, then shoves a cookie up right after it. How's that gonna help? says the guy. But the doctor just tells him to come back tomorrow. So the guy goes home, comes back the next day, drops trou, bends over, the doc sticks *another* egg up his butt, counts to fifty again, and shoves up another cookie. The guy's thinkin' of changing doctors by this time but the doc *insists* the guy come back for one more treatment the next day—money-back *double* guarantee. The guy can't pass up a good deal, so he comes back. Same thing—pants down, bottoms up, the doctor sticks up the egg . . . but this time he doesn't count. So the guy's waitin', waitin', he's just about to forget it, when suddenly the tapeworm sticks his head out the guy's ass and says 'Where's my cookie?'—and the doctor whaps it with a hammer. Cured."

10

Jordan laughed louder than he'd have liked, knowing it would oblige him to take at least some of the man's literature.

"And the moral is, doc," Abel smiled, "never turn down a good deal, and in medicine, patience is everything."

"Patients *are* everything, Abel."

"That's what I said, doc. Anyway, here, take this, a little something." He handed a shiny, monocle-sized object to Jordan. "Multifunction—it's got a blade-edged tube for doing emergency tracheostomies, calipers for EKG reading, a splinter forceps . . ."

Jordan opened the various tools, then folded them back into their neat little case. "Kind of a Swiss army hospital," he smiled.

"Precisely," said Abel.

Jordan pocketed the gizmo without another thought. "Thanks."

Abel beamed. "No obligation."

The next patient had fever and a stiff neck, and Jordan needed to find out if she had spinal meningitis (or "smilin' mighty Jesus," as the patient called it). This required that he perform a lumbar puncture. Spinal tap. Jordan had Playter curl the woman into a fetal position on her side. Then he located the fourth intervertebral space by drawing an imaginary line across the woman's back, connecting the wings of her hips, and where that line intersected her spine, Jordan sank his needle.

Delicately he advanced it, a quarter-inch at a time, angling slightly upward as he went in, aiming for the sac that surrounded the spinal cord, insinuating the six-inch-long needle between the third and fourth backbones. Jordan loved this procedure—the sensing of in-

11

ternal structures, the finesse of the manipulation, the final resistance, and then "pop" as the needle punctured the membrane and slipped into the fluid spinal canal.

Jordan was an ace at slipping in.

Jordan's next patient was Chessie. Francesca Lewis, the chart read. Made his chest constrict a bit as he walked to Room Two, thinking of all the ways he might enter—surprised, concerned, pleased, indifferent. No, not indifferent, she could see through professional indifference, and she could see through Jordan. This was Chessie Lewis.

"Chessie?" he said, mostly in just plain disbelief, before he even had the door completely open. But then there she was, and he stopped halfway into the room.

"Jordan," she said tentatively. She held her left arm across her belly, her right elbow in her left hand, her right hand to her face—two fingers against her temple, two against her nose, thumb at the angle of her jaw. But even postured in reticence, she was beautiful. Tall and raspberry blonde, yet her eyes were dark brown, almost black: Jordan's opposite. Opposite in temperament, too—to him, everything felt easy, while *her* life was filled with decisions, her decisions filled with ramifications. Jordan had breakfast; Chessie had fruit, two coffees, one cigarette. Everything mattered to Chessie; what mattered mostly to Jordan was Jordan, though at one time Chessie had mattered to him, as well.

He took a step toward her, opening his arms, as she extended her hand to shake. Awkwardly, he tried to cover his relative forwardness by dropping his left arm, as if merely to shake hands; but at that moment she brought up her other arm in a gesture of warmth, feeling suddenly much too formal . . . so they finally half hugged, half fell into each other, like two toddlers mimicking embrace.

"Long time no etcetera," Chessie half smiled.

"How the hell you been?" Jordan spoke quietly.

"Pretty good," she lied, poorly. "You?"

"Excellent." He lied well. "What are you doing here?"

"Just . . ." She shrugged, raising her hands, looking for where to begin. That's when he noticed her left eye. It was bloodshot.

"What happened to your eye?" he said.

She flinched as if he'd struck her; then twisted her lip sadly. "Billy hit me," she said.

Jordan tensed. "That disgusting piece of shit." Billy was Chessie's husband, the man she'd left Jordan for three years earlier. Jordan was a man who kept his cool and his counsel in most situations—surviving the daily battery of the emergency room depended on it—but the subject of Billy Lewis was always enough to ruffle him.

Chessie saw the red in his face, tried to mute it. "Jordan, please . . ."

"I'm gonna call the cops . . ."

"I already have." Her bitterness was underlined by the patience in her voice. "They call it a 'domestic beef.'"

"Then I'm going over there myself and . . ."

"Jordan, I'm leaving him," she said with a simple finality. End of discussion. "I've already left."

There had never been any arguing with her. She always had a thousand reasons for and against, but once she'd decided, she'd decided.

He began to examine her eye more closely. Left eye, oculus sinister. Conjunctival hemorrhage, he thought— a broken blood vessel in the surface of the white of the left eye—traumatic, but not serious. Extraocular move-

13

ments intact, pupils equal, round, reactive to light and accommodation, fundi benign, no retinal hemorrhages or exudates, venous pulsations good, no infraorbital tenderness or hypesthesia . . . basically a sound eye. No damage that wouldn't heal in a week.

"You got a place to stay?" he asked quietly as he peered closely at her iris.

"Staying with a girlfriend."

"When did he do this?" Trying to get a feel for how long she'd been putting up with the abuse, how long the woman he loved had been in pain.

"Last week. The eye didn't get red until three days ago, though." She sniffled, then laughed. "I think I got the flu, too."

He remembered the way her laugh sounded, and took her into his arms as the laugh took him into his memory. She let her head rest on his shoulder, breathed a great sigh. They were instantly half-together again.

"How long has this been going on?" he whispered.

"He's never hit me before," she said almost curiously, sitting up once more. "But his coke habit's been out of control for months . . ."

Jordan nodded. A familiar story, down here at Emergencies R Us. "Think he could stick with a rehab program?" He hoped not. He hoped the fucker would self-destruct.

Chessie's voice flattened like a wall. "He can do what he wants, now. I'm done with it."

Jordan felt shamefully pleased with this information, though he kept it to himself. He felt tender toward her, too, and protective; and his own neediness came rushing up. "How about dinner tonight?" He hoped he wasn't pushing.

"Think I'm swearing off men for a while," she smiled.

It was a smile, he saw it. "Well, then, how about a diet lunch?"

Her smile broadened, even relaxed. "Maybe a snack sometime."

He looked at the address on her chart. "This where you're staying now?"

She hesitated, understanding the intent of the question, understanding that her nod would be an invitation—for help, even for comfort and joy, of which she'd known little for over a year . . . but wasn't that why she'd come here now to begin with? Not for her eye, but for her spirit?

She locked eyes with him a long moment, sharing uncertainties. And then she nodded.

He treated his next several patients rather peremptorily, his mind elsewhere—on Chessie, primarily, but also on the theater tickets he had for tonight, and the girl he was going out with, Diana, herself a hot ticket. He didn't know why he was dating her, exactly, except to feel younger—she was half his age. Maybe that was reason enough. Suddenly Chessie's appearance made it seem insufficient.

At one o'clock Jill Fergus came down to relieve him for lunch. She was one of the physicians in the group that ran the ER, though today she was playing house doctor—a sort of free-floating doctor-at-large who troubleshoots on hospital patients who suddenly go sour, until their own private doctors can be located. It frequently amounted to bailing the private doctors' asses out of hot water, but there were long, quiet periods with nothing to do, as well—and when it was quiet, the house doctor generally relieved the ER doctor for lunch.

Jordan felt too distracted to eat, though he was glad

for the break. "Thanks, I'm on beeper five-zero-seven," he told Jill, pressing the button to make sure the batteries were good. "I'll be in the morgue."

Jill nodded, smiling. "Better that than the tuna fish in the cafeteria."

Russell Hall was the chief pathologist, and Jordan's oldest friend here. They'd done their medical internships together at County Hospital, and sharing battlefield conditions like that for a year made people either friends or enemies for life.

Hall was lanky, smirky, blond, and unflappable, and was just beginning an autopsy as Jordan entered the morgue.

"How's business?" said Jordan.

"Dead—which is to say, booming."

"Yeah, I heard we sent you a couple customers from the ER last night."

"Just this one." He indicated the mottled figure on the steel table before him. "The other one the family refused to sign for postmortem. Can't blame 'em, the guy was ninety-three, his number was just up."

He picked up the bone saw and turned it on. It made a high-pitched whine. He lowered it onto the cadaver's sternum, cutting through rubbery flesh, woody bone, caseous marrow.

Jordan watched the bloodless penetration in silence until Hall was all the way through to the heart. "I saw Chessie today," he said finally.

Hall took the information in thoughtfully. He'd known Chessie, too—eight years before, when he and Jordan were both residents and Chessie was a medical student. He knew Jordan's history with her and then

16

without her. "Saw her where? Around the neighborhood, you mean?"

"No, here—she stopped by to say hello." He tried to sound casual, but it didn't fool anyone else in the room.

"Oh, yeah? What's she up to?" said Hall, willing to play the casual game. "She ever go back and finish med school?" He cut out the corpse's heart, and tossed it on the scale.

Jordan shook his head. "Went into marine biology— does deep-sea videos now."

"Like for PBS or something?" He wrote down the heart's weight in grams and began to probe its recesses, feeling for clot, for hardening, for rupture.

Jordan shrugged. "She free-lances—has an office someplace down the marina." She'd told him that on her way out—invited him on a scuba tour of the South Bay, actually. He was skeptical, though—suspicious of any water that didn't have an ice cube floating in it.

Hall cut out the left lung, dense with congested fluid, carbon black with fifty years of cigarette smoke. "She still with What's-his-face, that jerk she married?" he said, flopping the lung onto the scale like a polluted fish.

"No . . . they're separated."

"Oh, yeah?" said Hall. He knew he was on the money. "So . . . you going to start seeing her again, or what?"

Jordan shrugged again. "I don't think so."

"Why not? You've suddenly got something against married women?"

Jordan's reputation as a lothario was old news in the hospital, but known intimately by no one better than

17

Hall. This was no grand adventure to Jordan, though. "Gimme a break, hey?"

Hall retreated. "Sorry. So . . . call her up. Life is short."

"Too short to go around *that* track again."

"So maybe you'll get it right this time around."

Things seemed to keep going around and around for Jordan, without getting him any closer to anything. Birthdays, Christmases, New Years, old years, relationships . . . the carousel of life. Time to change ponies again? He felt a sort of nebulous, free-floating anxiety, but couldn't name the fear, which meant he couldn't control it. And control was Jordan's big issue, as it was with most doctors: he needed to feel in control.

"What's this?" said Hall. He'd walked over to Jordan, and was suddenly peering intently at his neck.

"What's what?"

Hall pointed at a darkling freckle. "This nevis. You had this looked at? I think it's getting bigger."

In medicalese, nevis meant mole, but smacked of malignant melanoma.

"I think your eyes are getting smaller."

"I'm serious. Come on, I'll biopsy it this afternoon, you can start on chemotherapy tomorrow."

"Fuck you."

Hall grabbed the smoky lung from the scale and pointed it at Jordan. "You got your will in order?"

They were joking, as doctors do, about how we're all on the crumbling edge, one foot rocking while the other foot rolls, and no percentage in sitting out this dance.

But for Jordan, the punch line was about to punch.

CHAPTER 2

L one Ranger opened one eye: the day rushed in.
Light, shadow, sound. His senses were jangled,
as if by knifeblades to each part of his body. And
he was a man of many parts.

He sat up. Rubbed his hand over his chest, which had
no hair. To feel his own skin, a familiar touch. To know
he was in his own body. Once a week he used a de-
pilatory cream over his chest, legs, face, arms, head—to
erase all the hair, to bring his skin closer to the surface.
To make this first touch of the morning more immedi-
ate. So he would have no doubt who he was.

He pinched his left nipple until it hurt; until a tear
came to his eye from the pain. To wake himself up. He
touched a finger to the tear and tasted it. Salty. Also
familiar. Yes. It was he.

He stood. He walked to the full-length mirror on the
bathroom door, pressed his body to the mirror, rubbed
himself against the glass until he got an erection. Moving against his own image. When he was hard, he
stepped back, masturbated to his reflection. Came into
his own hand. Licked his palm clean. Salty. Also familiar. Yes. It was good.

Lone Ranger had never had sex with another person. He was a man of many parts.

He did a hundred push-ups, two hundred sit-ups. He showered, dressed. He left his apartment.

He ate at a sidewalk café, up the block; drank two espressos; smelled the wind. It was a good wind: potent. He inhaled deeply, held it within himself, sensing its notions.

He exhaled, full of a single notion: It was a good day for a kill.

By late afternoon Jordan had undergone several drastic mood swings, and was at the moment feeling rather pleased with himself.

Chessie had not come by accident; she'd wanted to see him.

And why not?

So *he* would see *her*, tonight, too.

And so what?

His birthday was in less than forty-eight hours— maybe Chessie was a present from the past.

He wondered where to wine and dine her this evening. He picked up the chart for Room Two from the rack, looked at the name: Dennis Breen. As he walked to Room Two, he noticed his pants, wondered if he should change before he went to see Chessie. Not enough time, probably, unless his relief showed up early. He hoped nobody would bleed or puke on his pants before the end of the shift. He entered Room Two.

"Hello, I'm Dr. Marks."

"Dennis Breen, doctor." Breen was a distinguished-looking man in a Brooks Brothers suit, fiftyish, seemed to know just what he wanted.

He wore an Ivy League tie, maroon with gold shields on it.

"What can I do for you, Mr. Breen?"

Breen smiled, like an old boy giving a peer the wink. "Actually, I'm just here to get a refill on my blood pressure medication—I've run out."

Jordan nodded, perusing the chart: Breen's blood pressure had been recorded by the nurse at 170/95. The top number—the systolic pressure—was in general a function of the force of the heart's contraction and the resistance put up by variably hardened arteries; while the bottom number—the diastolic pressure—reflected the plasticity of the blood vessels themselves, their state of capacitance or constriction, the pressure below which they would not fall. In Breen's case, the numbers were high on both sides of the slash. "And your own doctor's out of town?" asked Jordan.

"Actually, *I'm* out of town—I live in D.C., that's where my doctor is." Again, the intimate nod.

"On vacation here?"

"No . . . temporary job reassignment."

Jordan began taking Breen's BP to see if it was down from the nurse's reading. Guy looked Type A, in control but never off guard. Jordan tried to put him at ease. "Used to have a little blood pressure problem myself." He smiled, suggesting a confidence of his own. "The key is, you've got to learn to relax. What kind of work do you do?"

"Excuse me, you have a Kleenex?"

Jordan looked up from his stethoscope to see Breen tilting his head back slightly, blood oozing from his right nostril.

Jordan straightened. "Here, pinch your nose." He put

Breen's fingers around his nose, applied pressure, then pulled the otoscope off the wall and rummaged around in a drawer until he found a nasal speculum. He brought the light up to Breen's face. "Let me have a look."

Breen had taken out his handkerchief and mopped it all up, though. He waved Jordan off. "It's stopped already. It's nothing."

Jordan looked skeptical. "How long you had it?"

Breen shrugged. "Four, five days." He touched his nostril again: dry. "There, see, it's over." He pocketed his hanky. "Probably just a virus."

Jordan shook his head paternally. "Be rare for a virus to cause a nosebleed. Let me take a peek." He raised the scope.

Breen was quiet but unyielding. He clearly took a dim view of the instrument in Jordan's hand. *"Primum non nocere,"* he intoned.

Jordan laughed at the Hippocratic injunction: First, do no harm. He put down his tool. "Well, if you know your medicine that well, you know your nose is probably bleeding because your pressure's up."

Breen held up his empty medication bottle. "Then perhaps we could kill two birds with one stone if you wrote me a refill on my Diuril." It wasn't an order, exactly, but there was an edge to his voice now.

Jordan acknowledged the logic with a shrug and a smile, took out his prescription pad, and wrote.

"Thanks," said Breen, at ease again. "I like to keep my nose clean. And my septum deviated."

Jordan handed him the script with a comradely smirk. "You've obviously got a medical background." He looked at the chart again. "Let's see, you live in D.C.— you must be with N.I.H." National Institutes of Health.

Breen's eyes defocused as he put the prescription in his coat. "I used to be."

"What do you do now?" Jordan asked.

Breen looked up toward the corner of the room, as if there he might find the word he was looking for. And apparently he did. "I do consulting," he said, as if no further explanation were required. In any case, none was given.

At 7:10 P.M. Jordan exited the ER for the day, briefcase in hand, beeper on belt, pants unsullied, the night young. Everyone called and waved him good-bye, see you tomorrow, or the ever-popular gomer farewell, "O.T.D.A.M.F."—Out the Door, Adios Motherfucker. Jordan wished them a quiet night and walked into the main lobby.

There he stopped at a pay phone, deposited a quarter, and dialed. As the phone rang, Tracy passed by, also on his way home.

"*I'm* not in for a quiet night, sport. *I'm* comin' down with a bad case of boogie fever." Tracy grinned, shivered, and headed for the door.

Jordan called after him. "I hear Butterfield's playing at . . ." but then the phone was picked up at the other end of the line, and he spoke into it. "Oh, hi . . . Diana? Listen, I'm really sorry, but tonight is off, I just got beeped. . . ."

"Where, for Bay Cities?"

"No, out in the Valley, some moonlighter called in sick . . ."

"You're shitting me . . ." She sounded pissed.

He pulled his beeper off his belt, pushed the button to "Test" mode, and it beeped near the phone. Some stories needed special effects. "Listen, I gotta run, they're desperate."

"Maybe . . . later?" She wasn't sure how to feel.

"Yeah, if I get relief, I'll call. Otherwise talk to you tomorrow."

"Well, okay . . ."

"Bye-bye."

He hung up, feeling simultaneously low down and high. He didn't really want to hurt Diana, but he didn't really want to talk to her, either, about his recent developments. They'd have plenty of time for that later, if necessary. For now, it was all Jordan could do just to concentrate on looking relaxed when Chessie opened the door. This time, when it shut, he wanted to be on the inside.

The door opened.

A frizzy, petite blonde stood there, cigarette dangling from her lips, holding a pipe wrench loosely at her side. Loosely, but not casually. "Okay, what do you want?" she said. She held her voice the way she held the wrench.

Jordan took a step back. "Is . . . Chessie here?" This was the address she'd given, in Los Feliz, off Vermont, the lower rent area south of the boulevard.

"I don't know any Chessie."

"And I don't know you," said Jordan, "but . . ."

She started to close the door in his face, but then another hand came up from inside and stopped it. Chessie stepped into the doorway. "It's okay, Dolores. Jordan's a friend."

Dolores grudgingly stepped aside and motioned him in with the wrench.

It was a small two-bedroom apartment, the end unit

of a U-shaped complex of one-story bungalows. The front door opened just off the living room, which Jordan entered somewhat stiffly. All three of them remained standing.

Dolores spoke first. "Sorry," she said, not apologizing. "I thought you were one of Billy's spies . . ."

Jordan ignored her for Chessie. "You okay?"

She nodded. "Dolores is just screening all my 'gentleman callers.'"

Jordan's face tightened. "He hasn't threatened you again, has he?"

Dolores hefted her wrench. "The asshole's *existence* is a threat. To the *planet.*"

Jordan looked closely at Dolores's face for the first time. It was familiar, in an evocative way. No, not the face. The voice. "Haven't I heard you sing somewhere?"

She conceded, with reservation. "Sarno's, afternoons."

Jordan remembered now. She sang opera at a local bistro. She was pretty good. "You're pretty good," he said, nodding.

She almost smiled. "You want a drink?"

"Bourbon on ice?"

Dolores exited to the kitchen as Jordan and Chessie sat down on the couch. She put her head on his shoulder.

"I keep feeling like it's somehow my fault," she whispered.

"Because he victimized you? You don't have to buy that."

"I think he sensed I was leaving him behind. I was growing, he was just spinning."

"So now you're free. So chalk it up to experience."

25

"Experience is what you get when you didn't get what you wanted."

Jordan smiled. "Like med school, eh?"

"Med school was *several* experiences I got instead of what I wanted." She sat forward to reach her glass of brandy on the table.

Jordan laughed in his throat. "What was your favorite bad experience? Nyberg?"

"Nyberg was up there. The night he intentionally sewed that poor drunk's ear to the mattress and then screamed at me for having a bad attitude when I balked—that was medical school in a moment for me."

"Nyberg was a putz. In med school the most important survival technique was telling the putzes from the schmucks."

She shrugged. "One thing I learned: *Degustibus rectum porci fecum est.* The first law of medicine."

Dolores was just entering with Jordan's drink in one hand, the wrench in the other. "Which is?" she asked, handing Jordan the bourbon.

"'A pig's asshole tastes like shit,'" he translated.

"That's sweet, what's it mean?" Dolores hefted her wrench thoughtfully. She was obviously beginning to like the feel of it.

"It means," said Chessie, "that if you stick your nose someplace you know to be harboring certain foul and characteristic humors, it should not be surprising to find yourself recoiling from the smell."

Dolores nodded, understanding. "Or maybe coming up with a brown nose," she added, looking at Jordan.

"Hey, gimme a break," he said. "I just learned how to hold my breath sooner." He sipped his bourbon. "Or breathe through my mouth."

26

"And I decided I'd rather just breathe underwater," Chessie smiled.

"So what's that like, anyway?" he asked, shifting the topic to her tangent.

"Scuba? Like nothing else. The exact opposite of all the pain and noise and politics of the hospital and academic medicine. It's almost out-of-body, at its best—just this sense of you as a consciousness floating in this uniform, timeless ether. Almost not even 'you' anymore, like you're just part of this dark, fluid universe, all silent, and one . . . I think it must be what it's like when you die, and your spirit dissolves into space. It's too beautiful to describe, really. It's not like anything else in my experience."

"Sounds like the perfect drug."

"Only people in my life who use drugs," she quipped without humor, "are doctors and husbands."

"Bourbon only," he lifted his glass, "and only for medicinal purposes."

"I remember," she broke into a real smile at the shared memory: " 'Take two bourbons and go to bed with a friend.' "

They both laughed at that, then the laugh ended quietly, and left Jordan feeling even more manqué, somehow. When he looked at her now, there was real love in his eye, but real loss, too. He lifted his glass and spoke slowly, without singing: " 'Should auld acquaintance be forgot, and never brought to mind, should auld acquaintance be forgot, in days of auld lang syne, in days of auld lang syne, my friend, in days of auld lang syne, we'll take a cup of kindness, yet, in days of auld lang syne.' "

He drank. Chessie, moist-eyed, hugged him with feeling as Dolores pulled the drink from his hand in an effort to keep comedy out of the romance.

They pulled apart, and the room was filled with a slightly uncomfortable yet quite tender silence. Dolores played with her wrench. Chessie was obviously swaying under a crosscurrent of various emotions. And Jordan was more certain than ever of why he was here.

He pulled a torn newspaper ad out of his pocket. "Want to experience the Paul Butterfield Blues Band at the New Otani Hotel tonight?"

She shook her head uncertainly. "No, I couldn't . . ."

"Do it for me?" Jordan pressed. For auld lang syne.

"I don't think so," she protested, without much conviction.

"Do it for you, then."

Chessie smiled.

Dolores pointed the wrench at her. "Honey, you need to get your mind off that booger you left—and the first I've seen you smile since you got here is right now, so I'd say this guy on the couch is the way to go." She waited for a response from Chessie, but got none, so she rattled her wrench, and scolded. "So go for it."

Jordan flinched reflexively against the aggravated singer, but Chessie just grinned, stood, pulled Jordan up, and kissed Dolores on the cheek. "Don't wait up."

Chessie and Jordan left. Dolores stood in the foyer, watching the front door close, raised Jordan's bourbon to her lips, and toasted them. "Down the hatch." She clinked glass to wrench, and drank.

Lone Ranger loved to spy on people. It was like tasting their lives before he feasted on them.

The young man at the sushi bar was a perfect example. He was almost beautiful, but with a strange enough nose to be interesting; he ate salmon roe with quail eggs; he kept looking at his watch; he read the *Hollywood Reporter*.

Lone Ranger savored the nuances of the young man— the patient, impatient actor—the way some people relish old wine. Delicately, with a mixture of senses. And when the young man got up to leave the restaurant, Lone Ranger followed him.

He'd followed him all afternoon and into the early evening—from the bank to the audition, to the gym, to the sushi place. And now into the night.

To a series of bars, actually. The young man was getting high. Going into the bathrooms, doing a couple lines of nose-candy in one of the stalls, then sitting at the bar, having a beer. Probably to ease the low of blowing the audition, Lone Ranger guessed. It was weird to Lone Ranger the way every other dork in town was trying to break into Hollywood. Made things easier for him, though; always gave him an in.

Lone Ranger sat next to the young man in the third bar. "Hey—you're an actor, right?" Ranger pointed.

The young man looked sheepish. "Yeah—how'd you know?"

"You were in . . ." Ranger snapped his fingers, trying to remember.

"The Satin Plus commercial, you mean?" Pride, doubt.

"You were fantastic," said Ranger. "Fact is, I'm looking for someone with your qualities right now. Someone just your . . . flavor."

"Really? For what?"

"It's a period piece. Say, you fence?"

"Well . . ."

"Doesn't matter. You show up eight tomorrow morn-

29

ing, stage twenty-four, Burbank Studios, you got a job. Ask for Range." Ranger winked, slid off the barstool. "It's your lucky night, pal."

"Jeez, thanks . . ."

Lone Ranger left a five on the bar and walked out. He waited across the street only ten minutes before the young man emerged with a springy step, heading toward the beach. Ranger followed.

Three blocks later, Ranger stole up behind the young man, unsheathed a thin steel skewer, and plunged it into the boy's brain, entering from the rear, at the base of the skull, thrusting up from the back of the neck through the foramen magnum into the stuff of the hindbrain.

The young man stiffened, every body part in rigid extension, breathing stopped, pupils wide. Then Lone Ranger withdrew his needle and applied pressure to the puncture site with his thumb, so it wouldn't bleed, wouldn't stain the pretty New Wave curl at the tail of the young man's hairdo.

The young man convulsed a moment, drew a last, long breath, and lay still.

Lone Ranger whispered in his dying ear: "You got the part, kid. I never seen a better performance."

Then he kissed the young man's cheek and walked away.

Jordan and Chessie entered the lobby of the downtown hotel and followed their ears to the backbeat of the bone-shaking rock and roll that emanated from behind the double doors against the western wall. As soon as Jordan opened the door, though, the security man stopped them.

"Sorry, sir—capacity crowd."

Without missing a beat, Jordan steered Chessie down the wall of the lobby to a door thirty feet away, which had just opened and closed.

"What's this?" said Chessie.

Jordan shrugged. "I don't know. Sounded like a party, though." He ushered her inside.

It was a party. Cocktail party, well over a hundred people in formal attire, standing in twos and threes, drinking, laughing, talking.

"Pay dirt," said Jordan.

He led Chessie into the thick of it, grabbed a couple drinks from a passing waiter, gave one to Chessie, and stopped to face her as they reached the middle of the large, noisy room. He lifted his glass and looked around, and only then did he realize that everyone else here was Japanese. And speaking Japanese. He sipped his wine, smiled at Chessie. "So—you come here often?"

She laughed, a tinkling laugh. "I think you're a bad influence on me." She sounded greatly relieved to be laughing at all.

"If you just act like you belong somewhere, I find, people tend to accept it."

She shook her head, her eyes on him but far away, as if she were just remembering things about him. "You're still always trying to get away with something."

He kept his eyes fixed on her, and not far away at all. "Yeah," he said. "With you."

They ate a late night dinner at Gorky's. Caviar omelets served with avant-garde music, derrière garde paintings, dozing bums, and sleepless artists. In this milieu Chessie brought out her cigarettes—something she did either when she was at ease, feeling good, unthreatened

31

by person or circumstance or her own internalized shoulds; or, conversely, when she was anxious.

Jordan's eyebrows went up fractionally. "'It isn't the cough/that carries you off,/it's the coffin they carry you off in.'"

"Hey, gimme a break," she pleaded drily, and blew smoke in his face.

He fanned and coughed. "Hey, excuse *me* for trying to save your life . . ."

"I've managed to retain a few well-controlled vices into the eighties, so just leave me to them, if you please."

"Vice away."

"You've got a few of your own, now, I see—a silver BMW indeed. I thought all L.A. doctors drove Mercedeses."

"No, actually, there's a story about that, though— drug detail man at the hospital told me. True story. See, this mouse was walking through the jungle, and he happened upon this rhino trapped at the bottom of a pit . . ."

"A mouse and a rhino."

"And the rhino says please get me out and I'll do anything for you. So the mouse runs to the city, steals the best car he can—which happens to be a Mercedes—and drives it back to the jungle. He backs up to the pit, opens the trunk, takes out the chains . . ."

"What kind of chains?"

"Snow chains, what else?"

"In the jungle?"

"Near Kilimanjaro. Ski season."

"Say mid-July?"

"Thereabouts. So he hooks the chains to the bumper, then drops the other end into the pit, shinnies down, hooks the loops around the beast's horn, scampers back up to the car, puts it in first, and pulls the rhino out of the pit."

"It was a stick shift, then."

"Presumably . . ."

"How'd he work the pedals?"

"Platform heels. So the rhino says thanks very much, if I can ever do the same for you someday, I will. So off they go, and what happens but a week later the rhino comes to a pit in the earth, and who should be stuck there but the mouse. Will you help me? says the mouse. Of course, says rhino . . . whereupon he walks a few steps to stand *over* the pit, straddling it."

"A smaller pit, then."

"À propos a mouse."

"Less a pit than a hole, perhaps."

"A deep hole, then. A shaft, say."

"I could buy shaft."

"So the rhino closes his eyes and begins to fantasize— he imagines this horny lady rhino he's been wanting to rut with, rhino love, all that wrinkly skin getting tumescent . . ."

"She had a nice set of horns on her, I bet . . ."

"And what happens but his schlong starts to grow . . . and it gets longer, and longer, and harder, and pretty soon it's poking down the pit . . ."

"The shaft . . ."

"And it keeps growing until it reaches bottom, and then the mouse hops on and runs up it and escapes. And they both lived happily ever after."

"So?"

"So the moral is: if you have a big dick, you don't need a Mercedes."

She laughed gaily. "Jordan, you don't have a big dick."

He smiled apologetically. "BMW's all I could afford."

She held his hand. "It's a very pretty one, I must say, though."

"What, my car?"

She implored heaven. "Boys and their cars."

"Tell me now *you* don't have a fetish anymore. I suppose you don't brush a hundred times every morning and night. . . ."

And so it went—testing limits, memories; repressing, for a moment, everything except this table, this night, these faces. They were all over each other with their eyes.

Much later, he took her home.

They stood at her porch—Dolores's, actually—under a burned-out light, at the end of the talked-out date.

"I had a great time," she whispered. Her voice sounded as scratchy as her eye looked, and her eye was looking worse.

"I've missed you," he said.

They shared a long look; it seemed right. He began to kiss her. But she shied and pulled back.

"This is too fast for me, Jordan . . . right now. Tonight was lovely, but . . ."

He put his finger to her lips to quiet her—he didn't want to hear any disclaimers tonight. Then he kissed her affectionately on the forehead and walked back to his car. She went into the apartment and closed the door. He got in his car and drove off.

And watching them, slouched low in a car parked across the street, was a macho man in a sleeveless T-shirt, with a dragon tattoo on his arm.

And still further back, standing in the shadows of a massive bougainvillea, watching them all, was Lone Ranger.

Just getting a taste of things to come.

CHAPTER 3

Sometimes the emergency room was a mirthless crypt.

Sometimes the emergency room was an ugly but full-service resort hotel.

Sunday, December 29, 1985, at 2:10 P.M., the emergency room was a zoo.

Patients overflowed the waiting room, lining the halls, sitting on the floor, bickering for gurney space. Overdoses, chainsaw lacerations, bleeding ulcers, wheezing asthmatics, screaming kids, weeping bag ladies, litigious executives. Patient patients, impatient patients. Someone talking in tongues. Someone with mouth burns who'd tried to eat a live jellyfish. Someone who *had* eaten a tiny transistor radio, heavy metal blasting from his abdomen. A woman who claimed to have a rat in her vagina. A man with, in fact, a nest of spiders in his ear.

Phones were ringing, monitors beeping, oxygen flowing, tubes suctioning. Four nurses, three techs, and two doctors—Jill Fergus and Jordan—juggled ten jobs each, just to stay afloat, though it felt, at times, as though they were floating head-down.

Jordan, for example, was starting an IV on the diabetic

35

in Bed One, as he read the chest X ray on the bronchitis in Room Four, while he gave orders to Tracy about catheterizing the prostate patient in Room Seven, as he half listened to Gloria shouting a message from Dr. Theis, while another part of his mind registered the sound of an ambulance siren in the distance, while . . .

Jordan actually enjoyed these onslaughts, if they didn't happen too frequently. There was a sort of battle zone quality to them—a camaraderie, a doing-without-thinking, a recklessness of spirit—without the actual imminent fear of death. Though death was never far away.

And Jordan was a connoisseur of death. He'd battled it, observed it, made deals with it, prodded it, studied it, turned his back on it, danced with it, flirted with it, re-criminated it, balanced it, warded it off, led it on. Yet always a bridesmaid, never a bride: He'd watched death kiss so many, he felt like a professional voyeur. In the end that was all he could ever do—just watch.

And still, after all these years, he never understood it: One moment a man lay before you—sickly, ashen gray, afraid, but so alive—and a moment later, everything was exactly the same, every cell containing the same amount of sodium it had contained a moment before, every nerve ending touching in the same pattern, every-thing identical in its minutiae . . . only now the man was dead. Heart stopped, brain congealed. Jordan didn't get it.

But he kept watching, kept listening. Kept trying to figure out how to avoid death's kiss. Be death's virgin.

So he stared at the comatose diabetic before him, started the IV, gave him some dextrose, woke the man up. Death, begone.

Then he cocked his head to listen: He'd heard something. What, though? Some alarm or monitor? Was the asthmatic coughing again? No, it wasn't a sound; it was the absence of a sound. The ambulance siren outside had suddenly stopped.

Three things happened simultaneously. Jordan realized an ambulance must have just pulled up to the ER door; Cara hung up the phone and shouted that the base station had just called to tell them a full cardiac arrest patient was on its way via Rescue Ambulance 202, ETA five minutes; and the paramedics came bursting in, wheeling a gurney with a lifeless man atop it, doing CPR as they ran.

Jordan directed them to Acute Two. They transferred the patient to the bed, interrupting CPR only a few seconds in the process. Then a dozen things occurred in the space of a couple minutes.

Cara started a second IV in the guy's other arm. Tracy hooked him up to the EKG monitor. Jordan put a number eight endotracheal tube down his throat to control the airway, to bag his lungs more efficiently. Playter took over chest compressions, Tracy took over ventilation.

"What's the story here?" Jordan said, glancing at the ambulance report.

"Guy was found down a few blocks away," said Rogers, the burly paramedic. "Time we got there, he'd already blown his pupils." Blown pupils was medical jargon for pupils that were fully dilated, big and black. Blown pupils meant brain-dead. "No response in the field," Rogers went on, "he's had epi, bicarb, atropine . . ."

Jordan looked up at the monitor. "Okay, let's stop CPR for five seconds, see what we got."

All activity ceased: the group stopped pumping on the

victim's chest, breathing him, jabbing him. Everyone stared at the EKG tracing its green, luminous line: a wavy, meandering squiggle.

"Fibrillation," said Jordan. "Let's shock him."

Cara pushed the power button on the defibrillator; a red light began to flash on and off, blinking the word *Charging.* "How much?" she said.

"Two hundred," said Jordan.

Cara turned the dial on the portable machine to 200 watt-seconds—enough juice to electrocute a small mammal or, in this case, to try to jump-start a human heart.

She pulled the two paddles out of their slots. Metal discs with plastic pistol-grip insulating handles on them, they were connected by curling cords to the generator in the machine. And at the thumbside end of one handle, a small red button. Cara handed the paddles to Jordan.

He placed the metal faces down on the patient's chest—one high, over the sternum, one low along the left side. So the current would pass through the barely twitching heart, between the two electrodes.

"Everybody clear," Jordan commanded. Everyone stopped what they were doing, and took one giant step backward, to avoid touching the patient or the bed, which would have been equivalent to sticking a finger in a socket. It looked odd, though; like Simon Says Avoid the Reaper.

Jordan pushed the button on the paddle: The corpse jerked violently, then lay still again. Jordan looked up at the monitor. Nothing. "Flatline," he said. "Resume CPR."

The flurry of activity started in again. A characteristic odor wafted up to Jordan's nostrils: burning flesh. The carnal smell of defibrillation. It made him gag and sali-vate at the same time, atavistic responses over which he had no control.

The skin didn't always cook like that—in fact, it wasn't supposed to, if there was good, tight contact be-tween skin and the metal of the paddles. But if there was an air pocket—perhaps over the sunken flesh be-tween two ribs—or if the skin was wet with perspira-tion or alcohol . . . then a spark would jump. Arc between metal and tissue. And the crackling blue spark would cook skin and muscle.

Jordan couldn't eat meat for days after a poor-contact defibrillation.

Cara checked the patient's eyes. "Pupils still blown, Jordan."

"He's had atropine," Jordan shrugged. One of the drugs given to revive the heart, atropine also inciden-tally made the pupils grow wide. It was derived from the belladonna plant, called that because the señoritas of old would put it in their eyes to make themselves "beau-tiful ladies"—to make their eyes black with desire and allure.

Perhaps now it would entice death, for the final kiss.

Rogers just shook his head at Jordan's suggestion that the atropine was responsible for the pupillary dilation, though. "Bystander said he was down twenty minutes without CPR, doc . . ." He was telling Jordan to forget these heroics. The guy was boxed.

And Jordan knew it. Sometimes you just had to go through the motions, though. He tried a few more tricks—some Isuprel, some calcium, an intracardiac needle. Formalities. He looked at the EKG—flatter than Kansas. He touched the man's pasty white hand: a good thirty minutes cold. He hesitated, shrugged; thought of

39

another old med school dictum, the second law of medicine: *Fecum non carborundum*. You can't shine shit.

"Okay, let's call it," he said.

Everyone stopped. And then, as if the show were over and they were striking the set, they went about dismantling the corpse: disconnecting tubes and wires, emptying pockets from the man's half-opened clothes, turning off monitors.

Jordan just stared a long moment at the now official cadaver, as he always did at these times. Trying to clock the transition: not dead/dead.

Tracy caught Jordan's attention, and tipped his head at the corpse: "Hey, fuck 'im if he can't take a joke." This was Tracy the jester, suggesting the dead man was merely being a bad sport. Jordan broke his trance with death, smiled at Tracy's effort.

Playter, marking a document, looked over at Jordan. "Time of death?"

He looked at his watch: "Two thirty-seven." He walked up to the corpse's head, to make a final check on the pupils. He stared closely at the face, for the first time looking at the *man* rather than the parts that comprised him. And Jordan made a startling realization. "Breen!" he whispered.

"Say what?" said Tracy, preparing the shroud.

"This is Breen—I saw this guy here yesterday." Jordan felt shocked, though he wasn't sure why. "He came in with high blood pressure . . ." he noticed some crusted blood around Breen's nostrils ". . . and a bloody nose."

"Man, what'd you *give* him?"

It was another joke, but Jordan didn't think this one was particularly funny. He pulled open Breen's eyelids: The whites of his eyes were totally bloodshot, red with

40

hemorrhage. Conjunctival hemorrhage. It looked rather gruesome, and Jordan, for all his voyeuristic experience, felt a bit unnerved.

Cara, meanwhile, had rifled Breen's pockets—wallet, keys, papers—and now handed them to Jordan. "Personal effects. You want to call next of kin, or you want *me* to?"

Jordan neither looked nor felt thrilled by the prospect. "No, I'll do it," he said.

"Good," said Cara, and walked off.

This was the part nobody liked.

Jordan walked into his office, sat down, and dumped Breen's stuff on the desk. Then he pulled a death report and a large manila envelope out of a drawer. And then he began going through the wake of Breen's life.

The first thing Jordan noticed was the prescription for the high blood pressure medication he'd written for Breen the day before—Breen hadn't filled it. And so, obviously had not taken any of the medicine. "Jerk," thought Jordan, referring simultaneously to Breen for not taking the meds and to himself for not having given Breen a dose while he was here. He just shook his head now, though, and brought his pen down to the bottom of the death report, to the section labeled Diagnosis. He wrote:

1. Hypertension
2. Cardiac arrest

He went cursorily through Breen's wallet, found an In-Case-of-Emergency phone number, and pushbuttoned it on his desk phone. The beeps in the earpiece formed a familiar melody—Jordan couldn't place it at first, but then as the phone began to ring, he realized the number had sounded the first seven notes of "Mary Had a Little Lamb." He hummed, "It's fleece was white as snow . . ." and then the line was picked up at the other end.

"Hello?" said a woman's voice.

"Yes, to whom am I speaking?" Jordan asked. How you broke this kind of news depended on whom you were breaking it to.

"To whom did you wish to speak?" said the woman, her voice now subtly defended.

Plunge ahead with a soft lie. "I'm sorry, this is Dr. Marks, at Bay Cities emergency room—we have a Dennis Breen here who's seriously ill, and I was trying . . ."

"We'll be right over," said the woman, and hung up.

Jordan was a little taken aback, but hung up. No predicting people's reactions to the big D. People were stoic, people collapsed, people were thankful, or blameful, relieved, or disbelieving. People fainted, punched walls, punched doctors, wailed, wept, or walked away. Some people just nodded; some people just shook their heads.

Jordan's technique as messenger was to try to get the person he was telling to actually tell *him* the news. So he would say, "I'm sorry, I have some bad news, I'm afraid . . ." and the recipient of the news would say, "She's dead," and Jordan would nod as if he were just being told himself and to show the grieving party that at least one appropriate response was to nod. Also, if they said it themselves, they believed it quicker.

He gathered up all of Breen's personal things now and swept them into the large manila envelope, which he then sealed, and wrote Breen's name on . . . when suddenly, from out in the ER, came the shouts and crashes of a major scuffle, followed by the call of the head nurse: "Dr. Marks—come quick!"

Jordan jumped up and ran out, tossing the manila envelope on the cluttered desk. In his haste—there was a sickening thud outside, the sound of a body hitting a wall—he sideswiped the bookshelf as he exited, dislodging a stack of old journals, which slid off the shelf and onto the desk.

Burying the envelope.

Jordan went directly from work to Dolores's apartment. December 30, his birthday, was just five hours away, and he wanted some good company to defuse it. Maybe take Dolores and Chessie both out to dinner. There was a good nouvelle cuisine place nearby, he recalled, though he was fairly hungry. His friend Gary liked to joke that nouvelle cuisine meant "small portions."

He trotted up the three steps to the porch and knocked. The curtain beside the door parted, a face peered out; a moment later Dolores opened the door.

She leaned against the frame, cigarette between her lips. In her other hand she held a book she'd been reading, her finger marking the page. She regarded Jordan a little vaguely, neither unfriendly nor inviting, probably just into her book.

"Hi," Jordan beamed. "Chessie here?"

"Uh-uh."

"Oh . . . she was maybe going to meet me." Major deflation.

"She went back home." Pity crept into her voice.

"To Billy, you mean?" Shock, a hint of outrage.

Dolores straightened up. "Look, I don't like it either, but he called and begged her, so she went." Self-reproach now shaded her tone and her body language. "I shouldn't have let her stay here, she was too easy to find."

Jordan found himself unexpectedly wanting to comfort Dolores. Maybe just projecting his own disappointment. "She's a big girl, she can make her own mistakes."

Dolores shook her head. "She was too confused. You confused her more, I think. I think I should have protected her from you, too."

He stared blankly. "I love her." He didn't know he was going to say that.

"Easy to say," shrugged Dolores. "Billy said the same thing. Love is just . . . a device."

"So we're prisoners of our own device. So where does that get us?"

"Gets us life without parole, usually," she almost smiled, "and you just want Chessie to transfer to a new cell block."

He did smile. "You stretch your metaphors any thinner, you're going to get wet when it rains."

She laughed, once, a short whoosh of air through her nose.

"What're you reading?" he asked.

She turned the cover to face him. *The Art of the Audition.*

"I think optimism is the key," he nodded.

"That's what it says in chapter two. Seems to me that just sets you up for a bigger fall."

"I guess the trick is to know how to fall."

"Hard to do if someone's pulling you down."

He tired of banter. "You think she's okay?"

Dolores spoke like an actress describing a character at

an audition. "I think the arc of her life and the arc of her heart . . . don't coincide."

A funny smile suddenly twisted her face, almost an expression of grief. It spoke more directly to Jordan than anything she'd said.

"You love her, too," he said quietly.

Her mouth curled sadly. "I love her *better*."

Jordan just walked for a couple hours, among noisy crowds—he wanted to be alone, but with people. Up and down Melrose Avenue, first, its punk-chic stores open late, its impeccably mutant humans parading their orange and purple spiky coiffures with the more traditional leather and chains. Tonight, these legions of outcasts made Jordan feel right at home.

He went to Santa Monica Pier next. Rode the bumpercars, dissipated some bad energy. Rode the carousel in a Santa's sleigh, but just felt like the grumpy elf. Santa Claus of the Santa Anas riding the hot December wind in circles to midnight, when he would be a year older. A year closer to being next on death's dance card. Death was the one fear it never helped him to name.

Stop being so morbid, he thought. Have a drink, instead. He sat in the bar at the end of the pier and had several. He called his pal Russell Hall, for companionship, but only got Hall's phone machine. He recited the causes of eosinophilia into the machine and hung up.

He went home.

It was a condo in Marina Del Rey with an ocean view, a fireplace, a heavy mortgage: a standard young doctor establishment.

Jordan's decorative taste was more idiosyncratic,

though: an articulated human skeleton stood propped nonchalantly against the mantle; masks from around the world filled one wall; and telephones of every description were scattered around the room. Jordan was a phone freak.

An antique desk phone sat on the coffee table; a sleek burgundy cordless model rested in its own alcove; a fifties pay-phonebooth stood in one corner; a state-of-the-art three-line unit with call waiting, call forwarding, call anything, commanded the bar.

As Jordan entered the room, the Mickey Mouse clock-phone read 11:37 P.M. Twenty-three minutes to his next decade. He turned on a single desk lamp, poured himself some Cognac. He looked at his mail: ads, bills, a note from his lawyer, Nathan, about an upcoming deposition. He dinked around on his PC with an investment program he'd been meaning to try, but he was too moody. He replaced the disc with Missile Command, but immediately lost interest. He walked out onto the balcony, viewed the ocean, felt his insignificance fill its depths, felt how empty it left him. Empty of purpose, empty of love in his life. He sank into a sort of meditation of despair. Reminded himself of an old patient of his, Walter Glick, a man with chronic lung disease from thirty years of smoking cigarettes—Walter had a permanent tracheostomy hole in his neck from a previous bout of respiratory failure. The scene Jordan remembered now was this: in the dark midnight of a VA hospital, he'd heard a noise in the back room where all the old iron lungs were stored. He'd entered to find Glick crouching in the shadows behind a cluster of the silent, aging machines, his eyes sunken, his breath a long wheeze, puffing in secret on a Marlboro through the hole in his neck.

Jordan shivered away the vision—surely he wasn't

anything like that hollow man, so self-abnegating, lonely, alone . . .

He took another drink.

The doorbell rang.

He turned on the closed-circuit TV monitor to see who was down in the lobby. Flickering there on the six-inch screen in ghostly grays and whites was Chessie. Jordan buzzed her up.

She stalked past him into the living room without a greeting, and began pacing at once. Tense, upset. "I went home today," she said bitterly.

"So I heard." He tried not to load it.

"First he pleaded that I stay. I said I'd give it one more try. He said didn't I have any sense of loyalty. I said my sense of survival came first. That's when he took a swing."

"Are you hurt?" He looked with a doctor's eye, but he saw no bruises.

"I ducked, he fell, I ran. Been running all night."

"Me, too," he said quietly.

She didn't hear, she was all wrapped up in her pain. "He said running wouldn't help, though, said he found me once, he'd find me again. Said he'd kill me if . . ."

Jordan tried to grab her by the shoulders, to calm her down, to salve her wounds . . . but at his touch she lashed out, striking him across the side of his neck and ear, her agony suddenly galvanized into fury, as if his touch had grounded her pent-up charge. And as her fist connected, she whispered with a vengeance: "God *damn* his eyes, I'll kill him if I ever see him again."

He stumbled backward, knocking over the lamp, shattering the light into darkness. Momentarily, the force of her blow stunned them both; and then she fell, sobbing, into his arms.

He embraced her protectively, rocking slowly, giving comfort. "You're safe here."

"Did I hurt you?" she wept, touching the red welt on his neck.

"Only when you left," he said almost inaudibly.

She pulled away enough to bring her face up to his, and kissed him on the mouth. Warm, lingering, wet and salty with tears.

His legs felt like rubber. He folded to the floor, bringing her down with him. They locked around each other, mouths pressed and sliding. Trying to fuse. It got so intense so fast; he grew hard against her in an instant, they rolled into the couch, then back into the table legs, knocking something else over. And then her fingers were in his pants, pulling a sound from his throat; and his fingers were in her, wet as their kiss.

And the kiss deepened until they quickly lost all external sense, they were inside the kiss, tumbled within its slow, viscid pulse. Dark red, salty hot, full of her tears, too; and then somehow their clothes were off, the boundaries were gone, they were inside each other. Breathing underwater, rolling in the swells.

And then the kiss receded, like a warm saline tide, and they lay unmoving in each other's arms on the rug. It wasn't until the cool night breeze made them shiver, when their own heat had dissipated somewhat, that they rose, stumbled into the bedroom; and it wasn't until Jordan turned on the lamp to light their way that they really looked at each other's faces . . . and simultaneously gasped.

Their faces were covered with blood, smeared with it, some of it crusted dry, some sticky dark, some glistening; like primitive death masks, or the face-painting of a demonic ceremony.

Chessie backstepped, made a strangled sound. Jordan touched his own face, stared at hers in awe, at this physical manifestation of the metaphysical state they'd just shared. It took him ten, fifteen seconds to see the thin trickle of bright fresh blood curling out of her left nostril; to realize that Chessie's nose had been bleeding all the while they'd made love, and they'd been wiping the slippery exsanguinate all over their faces during the long, fluid passion of the kiss.

"It's okay, it's okay," he calmed her, "I'm your blood-brother now."

Then he had her pinch her nose as he got a warm washcloth from the bathroom to cleanse away the evidence.

He didn't have to be at work until noon the next day, so they slept late, and he made omelets for breakfast. Her nosebleed had stopped easily with pressure, but her eye looked, if anything, a bit worse in the fresh daylight. More bloodshot.

He rummaged around his medical bag for an ophthalmoscope with one hand as he flipped the eggs with the other. She said her eye felt fine, though; and in any case, he found his batteries were dead.

"Nothing dead about *your* batteries, child," she argued.

"You recharge me, my dear."

She shook her head, smiling. "Life is so strange. I mean who could invent this?"

"Please refer all questions to the manufacturer."

"Don't think I won't."

"I think the best approach to take is to think of life as a rather complicated, not entirely believable story, which is sometimes entertaining, and rarely instructive."

"So what can you do with that?"

"Just tell it," he shrugged. "Hardly needs embellishing."

"I just wish I knew which act it was."

"Second. It's always the second act."

"Yeah? When's intermission?"

"Why, you gotta pee?"

"Gotta blow my nose," she grumbled, wiping her nose with a Kleenex. "Damn flu."

"You never used to get sick, as I recall."

"I must be getting old . . ."

"My birthday!" he blurted.

"What?"

"It's my birthday today—and since you came over last night, this is the first I've thought about it."

"Your birthday—Jordan, I forgot, I'm sorry . . ."

"I forgot, and I'm not," he said. "I mean, it's a depressing time of year anyway, it's Christmas, and New Year's, and my birthday usually gets lost in the shuffle anyway, which is okay, since it's just one more reminder of my general decline toward mortality . . . but *this* birthday, *this* year, I don't know, it's just seemed particularly bleak, like I was getting particularly . . . auld."

"How old?"

"Forty."

"Sounds prime to me."

"Hardly. Divisible by two, four, five, eight, ten, and twenty."

"It's a good number, though. Has a lot of history attached to it—people walked in the desert for forty years, it rained forty days and forty nights . . ."

"I don't know," he shook his head philosophically, "it's the birthdays with zeros in them that do you in, I think."

"You're burning the eggs."

He flipped the eggs, and they ate; but try as he would, he couldn't get depressed about his birthday again.

He drove her to work near Redondo Beach—a little dive shop just off the docks, called Ahab's Basement. A hand-lettered sign in the window read:

> Charter Boats
> Scuba Rental
> Lessons
> Tours
> Scavenge

It was Monday morning, so the area was pretty quiet—a few old sailors tying bait, a few surfer kids playing hooky, a few shopkeepers opening up slowly. Jordan and Chessie held hands lightly as they walked, silent and content in the vivid sea breeze.

As they entered the little shop, the opening of the door rang an old ship's bell. The place was a chaotic jumble of fishing and diving gear, ancient carved wood figureheads, scavenged flotsam and jetsam of all kinds. Rusted trunks, barnacled anchors, broken swords, shredded nets, antique whaling harpoons, dented oil lamps.

A twenty-five-year-old guy came out of the back room, a shaggy blond, tan beachnik named Dave. He ran the place.

"Señora Francesca!" he smiled. He was the type who'd spent his entire life on the water's edge, and always would.

"Hi, Dave, got anything for me today?"

He went through a pile of scribbled memos on his desk. "Sure do—fella wants an expert to show him the Catalina reef . . ."

"That's my best thing, life at the bottom," she said with a droll sort of conceit.

Dave found the number, handed it to Chessie, and smiled at Jordan. "Hi. Dave Long. Can I help you with anything?"

"Jordan Marks. I'm with her."

Chessie looked up from her message. "I'm sorry— Dave . . . Jordan . . ."

"No problem." Jordan smiled. "I gotta run, anyway."

He took one of the store's business cards off the counter and put it in his pocket. Then he moved to the door with Chessie, as Dave sat at the desk.

"See you tonight?" Jordan asked. He didn't want to push. He wanted to sound optimistic, like at any good audition; but he didn't want to fall. And he knew if he pushed and she stepped aside, he would fall.

"I don't know," she shrugged tentatively. She obviously didn't want to be hurt again, but she didn't want to hurt him again either. "I think I gave up on Billy a long time ago—cut him off, to save myself. And I think you just made me realize it. I mean, this actual physically breaking away from him is a lot less painful than I expected, I've been emotionally gone so long. In fact leaving him now feels so easy, I almost feel guilty about it. And last night was so good . . ." She looked for words, didn't know where to go with it. "But I don't want to bounce from him to you. . . ."

He shook his head in accord, but not too vigorously.

She appreciated his restraint. "I think I need to get lost in my work for a while."

He nodded. "Sounds like a plan. Anyway, I'll be home, if you just want to talk."

Her eyes filled with tears, and she hugged him, and whispered, "It means so much just to know I can still love someone. That that part of me wasn't broken." He held her for a minute without speaking, until she finally backed up, touched his cheek. "Thanks for being with me like this."

He grinned. "I figure if I just act like I belong here, you'll tend to accept it."

She offered a lame smile. "I can't be a very fun party to crash right now."

"Just wait'll after the party."

"Okay," she said, "I will."

A couple hours later, as Jordan sat at the nursing station desk writing up a chart beside Jill Fergus, who was doing the same, he dropped his pen, left it on the floor, and stared into space. The ER was moderately busy, but he just stared for a minute, feeling distracted, as if he'd forgotten something, he wasn't sure what, his mind buzzing with so many other random impulses, tunes, shades of elation, memories of loss . . . and then the question just plopped into his brain, and he turned to Jill. "You been seeing more nosebleeds lately?"

She looked up from her chart. "What—you mean just ordinary epistaxis?"

"Yeah."

She thought a moment, shrugged, went back to her chart. "I don't know. Maybe one or two."

"What do you make of it?"

She didn't look up. "I just tell 'em to quit pickin' their noses."

He got up, laid his chart down, walked over to

Gloria's desk, stood beside her, and turned back the pages several days in the ER logbook. Gloria smiled seductively and put her hand high on the back of his thigh.

"Hey, Dr. Feelgood," she teased, "You can check my log if I can check yours."

He ignored her, though—he was concentrating on the diagnosis column as he ran his finger down it and turned page after page; and page after page, his finger came to, and paused at, the same recurring diagnosis: epistaxis.

A lot of people were showing up with bloody noses.

CHAPTER 4

L one Ranger was still hungry. He'd acquired a voracious appetite for human life in Vietnam, as a ranger; and since then, he'd simply never learned to diet.

His assignment in Vietnam had been to creep, alone, through the jungle, slip into an enemy camp at night, silently kill two or three soldiers—by knife, by garotte, by hand—and then steal away without arousing anyone. When the dead were discovered the next morning, fear—it was assumed—would paralyze the others, or cause them to run in the face of such potent magic.

It was during these close, night encounters that Lone Ranger began to learn the nuances of the odor of sweat—fear, fatigue, exertion, death, heat: They all smelled different, distinct. And they mingled, when he was in silent hand-to-hand with some perimeter guard, like the vapors of a complicated meal.

Understand, though: Lone Ranger was not one of those sad and latterly studied American boys who were twisted by that hopelessly murky war experience, unable to reintegrate into society, maladjusted by the violence and despair of Southeast Asia to a life of bitterness and nowhere to go. No—Lone Ranger had *volunteered* for his particular mission in the jungle. Lone Ranger had been a certified, violent psycho all his life. In Vietnam, he'd merely honed his craft.

He'd learned, for example, that in order to win a knife fight, you have to get in close enough that you *know* you'll be seriously hurt yourself. Over the years he'd been stabbed in the lung, in the liver, in the neck, in all his extremities—but these were not marks of courage to him, only of professional competence.

He'd learned technique—the needle in the brain, for instance.

He'd learned the value of instilling fear. Sometimes he wore lipstick during his midnight raids, and kissed his victims as they lay dying, so his lip imprint would be found by the survivors in the cold dawn mist.

And he'd learned to value his skills, as befits someone trained in a service occupation.

So now it was fifteen years later, and for the past ten he'd been free-lancing his services to a wide range of clients. And between jobs—to maintain his skills, and to slake his thirst—he jobbed a little for himself.

Stalking Chessie Lewis was a little of both.

She was, first of all, the kind of person he found just . . . to his palate: she seemed hard without being brittle; she used no perfume, so her essence could be appreciated, undiluted; and there was something about her that wanted to die. Ranger didn't know what it was, though, until Billy showed up at the door of the place she was staying.

Ranger hung back, watching, from a small grove of plantanos and bird-of-paradise plants across the street; so even though they were shouting, he didn't hear everything that was said. He heard enough to understand that Billy Lewis was her husband, though—and that made the little piece of death inside Chessie more readily comprehensible: Clearly, this man was her albatross.

For Lone Ranger, on the other hand, finding the two of them together like this was pure fortune.

"Go away," Chessie was telling Billy at the front door of Dolores's place.

"Honey, I'm sorry, you gotta believe that."

"I don't care what you are."

"I swear it'll never happen again."

"No shit." She started to close the door, he held it open, pulled her out onto the porch by the arm. "Let go of me," she said in a rising voice.

"I can't let go of you," he shouted. "You're inside my brain."

"Yeah, well there's not much else up there to get in the way, is there?"

"Stop laughing at me!" He pushed her against the outside wall.

She groaned and lunged at him. In setting himself for her blow, he backstepped, his foot inadvertently slipping down a stair, and he fell backward down the three steps to the ground.

Several units up the courtyard, the door opened and the manager stuck his head out to investigate the commotion. Chessie grabbed a potted cactus off its sconce and hurled it at Billy, who twisted to avoid it. It shattered on the walk near his head, sending pottery shards and cactus needles into his face. No serious damage, though. Chessie tromped back inside, slamming the door.

The manager continued staring at Billy until Billy stood slowly, shaking, and yelled at the manager, "What the fuck *you* staring at?"

The manager went back inside. Billy went back to his car and drove off with a screech.

Lone Ranger strolled from the plantano grove toward his own car, and toward the apartment building.

He was, for a moment, undecided.

On his break, Jordan ambled down to the morgue, where he found Hall doing an autopsy on a young woman—drug addict, by the look of the yellow purple bruises and needle tracks that ran up her arms, her feet, even her neck. Hall was dissecting her hand as Jordan walked up.

"Hi. Doing anything tomorrow night?" Hall said without looking up, picking apart two infected tendons.

"I don't know," Jordan responded noncommittally. "What's tomorrow night?"

"New Year's Eve, chief. Got your resolutions ready?"

"Just one."

"So bring her along."

"Where's the party?"

"My place—I don't have to drive home that way."

"I'll see. Might just opt for a quiet resolution this year. The resolution to all my woes."

"What—you got it together with Chessie already?"

"You have pretty good clinical acumen for a pathologist."

"Say, you move fast, man. That's no resolution, that's a resurrection . . . at least it's *some* kind of 'rection." He opened the joint-capsule in the corpse's hand, where the ring finger met the palm. Pus drained out.

Jordan watched with mild disgust, but something else

was on his mind. "So what'd you find on Breen's autopsy?"

"Breen? There was no autopsy."

"What do you mean?" Jordan felt the earth wobble slightly.

"I mean his private doctor showed up down here—guy named Harris—with a telegram from the family. Refused postmortem and left with the body."

"But the law *requires* autopsy on anyone dying in the ER." Legally, on anyone dying within twenty-four hours of admission to the hospital, it was an automatic coroner's case.

"Not if the private doc has seen the patient within the last month, and is willing to sign the cause of death—which this guy Harris did." In point of actual fact, the coroner's office loved it whenever a private doctor was willing to sign such a death certificate without autopsy, even if the patient *hadn't* been recently examined by the doctor—the coroner was so swamped with cases as it was, there was a six-week backlog on autopsy-proven cause of death. Any kind of relief they got on new cases was as welcome as a breath of fresh formaldehyde.

"So what did this Harris guy say?" asked Jordan.

"Stroke," Hall said, as if the conclusion were foregone. "Blood pressure out of control, bled into his brain."

"Makes sense, I guess," Jordan concurred. "Bleeding into his nose, when I saw him."

"There you go."

Still, something was out of place. "But I thought his private doc was back in Washington." That was why Breen had needed a new prescription from Jordan.

"I wouldn't know about that," Hall mumbled. He was swabbing the pus with a Q-tip and plating it out on a culture dish.

Jordan tried to piece together threads that didn't match. It just left him feeling threadbare. He kept picking at the loose ends, though. "Been seeing a lot of nosebleeds lately, I think. You know of any *infectious* causes of epistaxis?"

"No, but if you're curious, I know a guy over at public health, Art Reingold, he might know. He's in communicable diseases."

Jordan walked over to Hall's desk in the corner of the morgue, flipped through the Rolodex, got Reingold's number, and called. "Dr. Reingold, this is Jordan Marks, over at Bay Cities. I got your name from Russ Hall."

"If you're selling disability insurance, I can assure you—" Reingold began.

"No, no," Jordan interrupted, "I'm an ER doctor."

"Ah, well, then," Reingold's tone mellowed. "What was it you wanted?"

Jordan jumped right in, actually more curious than anything else at this point, now that he had an expert on the line. "Well, I've been seeing a lot of epistaxis lately, and I was just wondering if you have any recommendations."

"Sure," said Reingold, "tell 'em to stop picking their noses." He laughed.

Jordan chuckled politely. Everyone's a comedian, he thought. "Well, I was thinking it might be infectious, actually. . . ."

Reingold sounded more official now, more academic. "Don't know of any bacteria that cause nosebleeds, per se."

"What about viruses?" Jordan prodded.

"No . . ." Reingold said thoughtfully. "Some strains of echovirus can cause *conjunctival* hemorrhage, sometimes. . . ."

"Bleeding in the eye," Jordan said. The conjunctival membrane covering the surface of the eye, actually. The kind of problem Chessie was having, for example; or, more severely, the kind of bleeding Jordan had seen in Breen's eyes, as the man lay dead on the gurney.

"Conjunctival, that's what I said," Reingold repeated, as if to a dull student.

Jordan felt his pulse quickening. "Well if I *were* witnessing an echo epidemic . . ."

Reingold strained to keep the impatience out of his voice; he was, after all, a public servant. "Listen." He spoke as if diagramming a sentence. "I've got a new AIDS outbreak on my hands, we're trying to isolate a batch of bad Mexican cheese, my best fieldworker just had her gallbladder removed . . . I don't want to rain on your discovery, doctor, but there's just no way I've got the resources to follow up on a rash of nosebleeds."

"Right. I see your point."

"Sorry I couldn't be of more help." Interview over.

"Me, too," said Jordan. "Thanks anyway. 'Bye."

"Good-bye."

They hung up. Reingold really did sound sorry, but he also sounded awash under waves of communicable disease. Leaving Jordan once again on his own, and more unsettled than before. He walked back to the autopsy.

"Learn anything?" asked Hall.

Jordan tugged at his lower lip, mulling it all over. "Did you know echovirus can cause conjunctival bleeding?" he said.

61

Hall smiled. "No, but did you know echo is an acronym for Enteric Cytopathogenic Human Orphan virus?" He turned the cadaver's dissected hand over, filleted palm down, revealing an exquisitely julietted set of glossy red fingernails, which he now seemed to notice for the first time. He lifted one of the cold, stiff fingers toward Jordan, and said, "Beautiful nails on *this* human orphan, hm?"

When Jordan got back upstairs, he went directly to the ER log and retraced the past week for the diagnosis of conjunctival hemorrhage.

It came up five times.

He grew more nervous, though intellectually he felt he had no reason to be. Say something was going around. Big fucking deal. Flus went around all the time. And if Breen had caught it, too, well, he still died of a stroke related to his hypertension, his high blood pressure. A cerebrovascular accident, a CVA.

Jordan pulled Chessie's chart from the file, got Dolores's phone number from it, and called. He just wanted to hear Chessie's voice, hear that she was okay. Dolores answered on the third ring.

"Hello."

"Hi, Dolores? Jordan. Is Chessie there?"

"No, I thought she was with you, she called to tell me she left Creepo for good this time."

"Yeah, she *was* with me, I just thought she might be with you, now. I dropped her at Ahab's this morning, I'll try her there."

"Okay, any message if I talk to her first?"

"Yeah, tell her . . ." Tell her what? That she doesn't have influenza, she has echo? That she shouldn't forget to take her high blood pressure medicine if she gets high blood pressure? "Just tell her to call me," he said.

"Sure. And by the way," she added, "if you had anything to do with peeling her away from that slimehead . . . thanks."

"Sure. Take it easy."

"So long."

As soon as they hung up, he took the Ahab's Basement business card out of his pocket and began to dial. But he stopped midway when the paramedics casually wheeled in a dead body, halting the gurney directly in front of Jordan. He stood up, approached them.

"DOA," said Chaney, "you just need to pronounce him."

"Guy's got rigor mortis already," said the other paramedic, Sloan. This was a different pair than the ones who'd brought in Breen.

Jordan lifted the sheet. Lying there cold as matter was a macho man in a sleeveless shirt, with dragon tattoo on his arm. His eyes were wide open, and the whites were bright red with conjunctival hemorrhage. There was blood crusted around his nostrils.

Jordan gasped, and visibly jumped.

"Weird, huh?" said Chaney.

Cara walked up, a look of concern on her face. "Jordan, what is it, are you okay?"

But it wasn't the presentation that had stunned Jordan—not entirely, anyway. It was the person. "That's Billy Lewis," he whispered. "That's Chessie's husband."

He called Chessie's house, got the answering machine. He called Ahab's, but Chessie wasn't there. He called Dolores's, but nobody answered. Why didn't anybody answer? He felt shaken, but unsure of what was going on. Anxious about Chessie, her proximity to all this disease. He pulled Billy Lewis's medical records, determined that no doctor had seen him on a regular basis within a year. Jordan asked Jill to cover for him again, and wheeled the body down to the morgue.

"You owe me," Jill called after him.

He demanded that Hall do the postmortem immediately, abandoning the dead addict with the infected hand and the beautiful nails.

"Sure," said Hall, "she's not going anywhere fast."

First, he looked carefully at Billy's skin, the entire body. "Got some bruising around the face, little cut here, the crusted blood, of course . . . and this is interesting . . ." He got a forceps, pulled two tiny spicules from Billy's cheek and dropped them in a petri dish, setting the dish beside his microscope.

Then he opened the corpse up, neck to pelvis, and weighed and studied all the organs, looking for clues to the death, as Jordan sat there perusing Billy's old records. No clues anywhere. Hall did the head last. Jordan began to pace.

"Do a tox screen," said Jordan, "Chessie told me he was a cokehead."

"We *always* do a tox screen, chief."

"That could explain the bloody nose, too, if it was a coke overdose."

"Sounds like you got bloody noses on the brain."

"I told you, I think something's going around."

"Yeah, something's going around, Breen had a nosebleed from hypertension, and this guy here did like it says in the song, he blew his nose and then he blew his mind, probably on coca, and what's going around is, everybody dies sometime." He drew his scalpel deeply along the frontal hairline, from ear to ear, and peeled down the face, exposing the skull.

Then he continued his cut, finally pulling off the entire scalp, like a hairpiece. Then he turned on his bone saw, whining it around the top of the head. The smell of bone dust filled the air, pungent, like smouldering greenwood.

Hall lifted off the cap of skull, and there sat the brain: plump, gray, recently warm, now thoughtless. He cut it from its moorings, lifted it out, weighed it, sliced it thick, like sweet bread.

Jordan combed the chart again. "Used to be a pretty healthy guy, just a few sports injuries. . . ."

Hall examined the brain slices. "Cause of death looks to be cerebral hemorrhage."

"There's just no good reason for that. Even cocaine . . ."

"Now here's something odd."

"What?" He was only half listening, delving into the chart again.

Hall was sticking a probe through the core of the bloody brainpan. "There's a kind of linear pattern to this hemorrhage, seems to go back this way. . . ."

Jordan pointed to the last page of the chart. "Look at this—he came into the ER with epistaxis last Tuesday. What's today?"

"Monday." He put down the brain and began inspecting the back of the corpse's neck. He suddenly looked amazed. "Hey, look at *this*—a puncture site at the back of the neck."

Jordan walked over, all in a dither about his documentary discovery and its obscure meanings, but jolted now by what Hall was saying—and it was so hard to take anything Hall said seriously, Jordan was doubly confused. "What?"

Hall was controlled, quietly excited, pointing to the base of the cadaver's head. "Looks like somebody rammed a long, thin needle up the base of his skull, through the foramen magnum, and into his brain."

"What?" Jordan repeated, incredulous.

"Pithed him." Hall's look turned slowly, now, to one of professional interest. "I believe we have a homicide here."

CHAPTER 5

Jordan drove to Ahab's Basement, but was told Chessie had left hours ago. He drove to Dolores's, but nobody answered. He went to Chessie's house—the place she'd shared with Billy—but it was likewise silent. Silent as Billy.

And Jordan rode an undercurrent of fear during these searches; he was afraid for Chessie's well-being, and—naggingly—afraid Chessie had done it. Killed Billy.

Her motive was strong enough, certainly; and justified enough, as far as Jordan was concerned. What concerned him most now, however, was that he knew Chessie had the *skill* to kill Billy. Jordan distinctly remembered supervising her during her sophomore year, before she'd quit, at a dog lab, set up to teach clinical skills.

The dogs were pound animals, scheduled for euthanasia before the med school bought them. In the lab, they were anaesthetized, and then used as "teaching material" for the med students; tubes were put in the beasts, and taken out, and put in again, until the kids got it right. Chest tubes, nasogastric tubes, endotracheal tubes, suprapubic tubes. The kids learned how to defibrillate the doggies' hearts, shock them with the paddles; stick needles into their jugular veins to test central venous pressure; stick needles into their spinal canals to test spinal fluid—or, if the spinal canal was inaccessible, because of scoliosis or doggie arthritis, then the students were taught to needle the cistera magnum, where the cerebrospinal fluid was an easy mark . . . right at the base of the skull.

Jordan had this image in his mind, now. The students probing with their needles, the mangy dogs on respirators. And Chessie, standing there crying because she couldn't make herself do it.

Or was she crying because she'd done it once, with the needle, and then hated herself for it, couldn't do it again, wouldn't do it again?

The dogs were "sacrificed" at the end of the day. Euphemism for killed.

By the end of the next day, Chessie had left school.

Jordan wondered now just exactly how much Chessie hated Billy. Jordan was never a great fan of dog labs, himself; he couldn't really let himself think about them too deeply. But then, life was a compromise, was it not? Accept some bad, to generate some good. Even, perhaps, *generate* some bad, to generate more good.

And life was experimentation, was it not? Effect, observe, analyze, know. And to know—*that* was the most important thing. Was it not?

He wanted to know if Chessie had killed Billy. Truly, he doubted it and if she had, he supported her in it; but finally, he wanted to know.

It was late afternoon as he pulled up in front of Sarno's, on Vermont. The low clouds were peach and orange, underlit by the sun, which was itself beneath the line of the cityscape, in its decline. The sky was gray blue. Another long designer sunset over southern California.

In the hills just to the north, Jordan noticed the Griffith Park Observatory, its three greening copper domes obscured by haze, which meant, Jordan thought, that the hot, dry, dusty winds that blew in off the desert this time of year, the Santa Anas, had stopped. The evening would be cool.

He put a quarter in the parking meter and entered the small, dark café. Candles flickered on the tables. The waitresses all wore black—leotards, skirts, dance shoes—as if this were a perpetual bohemian grotto, frozen in time. Jordan took a booth near the back.

A heavyset man stood at the tiny piano, sipping grappa, singing intermittently some melancholy Italian operatic interlude. At his side, an older man filled in at the piano—without training, it sounded like, but not without soul—and wept and nodded as his friend sang.

There were only a few other patrons at this time of day. Nursing cappuccinos, talking in whispers, reading. Jordan looked up as Dolores appeared at his table. She wore the de rigueur black ensemble, with a black sweater covering her torso as well: She seemed chilly, or maybe just guarded.

Jordan smiled, trying not to appear as tense as he felt. "Have you talked to Chessie yet?"

"No. Have you?"

"No." He picked some melted wax off the candle, rolled it between his fingers.

"What's wrong?" said Dolores. "You look funny."

"So do you." He smiled. Joke.

"Ha ha, thanks a lot. You come in here to insult me, or you want a drink, or what?"

He paused, wondering how to say it. I'm sorry, there's some bad news, I'm afraid? "Billy's been murdered."

"What?" Like she didn't get the joke.

"Billy Lewis, he was brought into the ER, DOA, and the autopsy looks like murder."

"You're kidding."

He was watching her closely. It looked like real surprise, real horror. "The police are going to want to question Chessie, most likely . . ."

"No way," she cut him off. Protective, defensive.

"I want to talk to her myself," Jordan pressed on. "I don't think she did it," he didn't exactly lie, "but I *do* think . . ."

"Scum is better off dead, anyway." Relief had entered her voice, now, and vindication.

Jordan walked around it. "But I *do* think she may have some weird disease."

"What kind of disease?" Her voice took on a hush.

He wasn't sure how much he should tell her. "She's been . . . bleeding. Her eye, her nose . . ."

"That doesn't sound too serious." But she didn't sound too certain.

"It may not be. I've been seeing other patients with the same thing, though—some of them in worse shape than Chessie."

"You mean the bleeding's worse?"

He tried to shape his answer for her. "Ordinarily, simply the volume and rate of loss of blood will tell us how severe the problem is. But occult bleeding, or bleeding in a closed space . . ."

"What's that? Talk English."

"Occult just means hidden—you can't figure out where it's happening. Even a little closed-space bleeding can do a lot of damage, because there's no place for the blood to drain off, so pressure builds up real fast—like inside the skull."

"What do you mean 'inside the skull'?" she demanded. "You saying Chessie is bleeding inside her . . ."

"I'm not saying anything." He shook his head, groping. "I just need to see her." He spoke these last words completely undefended, without guile, like a child who's uncertain if he's lost, but whose mother isn't in sight. He just needed to see her.

Dolores looked hard at him, assessing his intentions. She took a red matchbook from the pocket of her black skirt, along with a half-empty pack of cigarettes, and lit up. As she exhaled, she seemed to relent. "Well . . . I might have an *idea* where she is."

"Tell me," he whispered urgently. He tried to make her understand his sympathies by the intensity of his gaze.

"It's like an underground network of women," she conceded. "They hide other abused women. . . ."

"So you know who she's staying with?" His face broke into hope.

She shook her head, though. "I just know the name of my contact," she explained, "and she knows the name of *her* contact, and so on and so on. Like a spy ring, sort of. And Chessie is somewhere down the line."

"What the hell is she acting like a fugitive for?" He was angry at Chessie for being in danger.

Dolores's voice rose. "Because her maggot husband was following her around with the intention of caving in her skull." Heads turned, Dolores chewed her lip. Jordan nodded, frustrated.

"When did she go into hiding?" he said more softly. If

they could prove it was before Billy's time of death, they were clear.

"Early today. Noonish, I think."

"Okay, okay, we're okay, I think. So you can call your contact, and get a message to Chessie to meet us at your place?"

Dolores nodded. She was still uncertain about him, but she could hear the relief in his voice. She said, "I'm gonna go to the morgue first, make sure it's really Billy. Chessie'd want to know I saw him dead, it's not just some scam."

Jordan felt hurt, but buried it. "Who *is* your contact, by the way?"

Dolores smiled for the first time, almost coyly. "Someone I see every night at bedtime."

"You don't mean Chessie?" Jordan pressed, confused. She shook her head. "Just an old drinking buddy."

"But a *woman* buddy, you mean . . ."

"Forget it, Ace," she cut him off. "I'll let you know."

It was heavy rush hour when Jordan drove downtown, and he made the additional mistake of taking the freeway so he remained nearly at a standstill for twenty minutes at the monster nexus where 101 met 110, 5, and 10, until he was finally dumped out at Sixth Street. He got to the County Building at 5:45 and parked in the red No Parking zone right out front. Too late to hunt down a pay garage.

He pulled an old parking violation ticket out of the glove compartment and stuck it on the windshield, under the wiper. He was a great believer in the concept that small sins were permissible in the service of pressing need.

He ran up the steps of the building, found the elevators. He felt like a salmon going upstream against the

72

flow of county employees leaving work for the day. Reingold's office was on the fourteenth floor.

Jordan knocked on the open door on which were stenciled the words Dr. Arthur Reingold, Communicable Diseases Section. Reingold, bustling around the filing cabinet, looked up momentarily, waved Jordan in and continued doing what he was doing.

Thirty-fivish, wearing rimless glasses and a bow tie, Reingold looked like an energetic Indiana academic. The office was filled—crammed—with books, piles of journals, filing cabinets, a computer terminal and printer, and reams of printout overflowing every available surface. The walls, however, were covered with old film noir movie posters. So, thought Jordan—an academic, but also a cynic, which is really just a lapsed romantic.

Jordan smiled. "You Dr. Reingold?"

"Depends what you're selling." Definitely a cynic.

Jordan extended his hand. "Jordan Marks, I called earlier about . . ."

Reingold brightened. "Hello, hello, Art Reingold, of course you called, I was going to call back, too, but you didn't leave your number."

"You find something out?"

"Well, I did get a call from the CDC in Atlanta, giving me a hotline number for inquiries about epistaxis." CDC was Center for Disease Control, the federal epidemiology watchdog. "There apparently *is* an outbreak locally," Reingold continued, "similar to one they're following in Florida . . ."

"Does it sound serious?" Jordan cut in. "Like any . . . complications related to the nosebleeds?" Or did two people with the epistaxis/conjunctivitis problem just happen to die of two different things?

"That wasn't my impression, that it was serious."

Reingold stuck out his lower lip. "But let's give the hotline a jingle—I'm curious myself now." He picked up his telephone, extracted a scribbled number from the pile of memos on his desk, and began pushing buttons. "Pick up on line two," he instructed Jordan, almost as an afterthought.

Jordan went to the wall phone, grabbed the receiver, and put it to his ear as the line began ringing. It was answered on the third ring by a woman.

"Hello?"

"Yes, this is Dr. Reingold at public health, I've got a Dr. Marks in my office here, with some questions about the epistaxis epidemic."

"Well, it's not really an epidemic as such," said the woman, softly patronizing. "We think it may be a dry-air problem, related to the extreme Santa Ana wind conditions, or possibly related to sunspot activity."

"You don't think there's an infectious cause?" Jordan broke in.

"Not that we can find." And if she couldn't find it, her voice was saying, forget it. "But we *would* like to send you some forms," she went on, "to report the cases you've seen. If I could have your name and address?" She sounded almost enticing, now; and almost familiar to Jordan. That tone of voice.

"Dr. J. Marks, Bay Cities ER, somewhere on Lincoln Boulevard, Bay City, California, nine double zero something something." He could never remember the exact address.

"Thank you, doctor. We'll be in touch."

"Right."

They all hung up.

Reingold shrugged, a sort of half apology for his public-health peers. "Well, the brain is a hollow organ, and none so hollow as those in charge of forms."

Jordan nodded. "Didn't shed much light, did she?"

"Light, I find, has to be self-generated if you want to see anything. Too many dim wicks floating around."

Jordan filled Reingold in on the details that had struck him—the nosebleeds, the deaths—then held his hands out in soft entreaty. "So—you got a light?"

Reingold took his glasses off, cleaned them. Jordan picked up an old leather book from his desk. *Contemporary American Poetry.* He opened it carelessly to the book-marked page, glanced at a few lines. "Prufrock . . ." he muttered, his memory stirred from the ashes of some long-forgotten college course.

Reingold smiled, closed his eyes as he put on his glasses. " 'Let us go, then, you and I . . .' " he quoted. Then his smile faded. He looked as if he felt he'd let Jordan down. And besides, his interest did seem piqued, as if perhaps some of his medical hunches had started out slimmer than this one and paid off. One of Reingold's personality traits, Jordan sensed, was that he could never let sleeping discussions lie. "Tell you what," Art volunteered, "I'll run it through our computer tomorrow—see if any other stations around the state have been plagued with bloody noses."

"I appreciate your help," Jordan said.

"Well, it won't take a minute, really."

"Frankly," Jordan confided, "I hope it turns out to be sunspots."

"Not much of a paper in that," Reingold's eye drifted to a point in the distant future, his Nobel Prize in medicine balanced delicately upon a pile of monographs reaching to the sun. Then he grinned at Jordan with a gentle, self-effacing twinkle. "We'll never make it into the *New England Journal of Medicine* with sunspots."

Jordan went back to Dolores's. No one home, damn her. Come on, come on. He vacillated a minute, then drove over to his favorite pub and hunkered down for some serious brooding on his birthday night. Random cuts from Prufrock drifted, unbidden and unwanted, through his mind, to litter his brainpan. *I grow old . . . I grow old . . . I shall wear the bottom of my trousers rolled.*

So okay, so Chessie had threatened to kill Billy, and now Billy was murdered. So Billy and Breen had both had epistaxis and conjunctival hemorrhages before they died. So Chessie had epistaxis and conjunctival hemorrhage. So she was going to die. So, Jordan was going to die, too, he was already forty years old, for God's sake. He grew old, he was old.

It reminded him of when he was in medical school, and all the students used to get every symptom that came down the pike. Reading about *hypo*thyroidism this week? You'd say yeah, well I'm tired, and I'm putting on weight, and my voice is getting kind of hoarse . . . my God, I haven't got *enough* thyroid. And then the next day you'd be reading about *hyper*thyroidism, and you'd say yeah, I been feeling kind of weak, and my pulse is a little faster lately, and my hair is definitely thinning in front . . . my God, I've got *too much* thyroid.

So then you knew it was okay, you were just trying to fit syndromes to random symptoms.

So maybe that's what he was doing now—maybe nothing was really going on at all. Just a dose of mid-life crisis, sensitized by the appearance of an old flame on a birthday with a zero in it. Just a little hypo-hyper-existentialism. He suddenly saw his mortality nearer than far, and suddenly death was everywhere.

Reingold, after all—the expert in communicable diseases—seemed to think this was at most an insignificant little event, of academic interest if other matters had not been more pressing. And Hall—the expert in death—seemed to think the only point of interest was the needle hole in the back of Billy's neck.

Which brought Jordan back to Chessie again. He couldn't believe she'd killed her husband. He didn't *want* to believe it because he wanted *her*, and if she'd pulled a stunt as obvious as that, she was sure to get caught.

But God, he wanted her. He remembered how he used to try to impress her on rounds, spinning off differential diagnoses as if he'd written the book. Trying to get her attention.

Maybe that's what he was doing now, just trying to get her attention by inventing new syndromes to fit around a cluster of random symptoms. He knew he was a storyteller, after all. Maybe he was a Munchausen, as well.

People with Munchausen's syndrome were confabulators. They invented symptoms, they *created* painful symptoms and even dire illnesses in themselves, just to get medical attention, attention from doctors and nurses. Maybe Jordan was creating syndromes and illnesses in *other* people, so *he* could garner some attention from Chessie. Wouldn't be Munchausen's syndrome, exactly, then. More like pseudo-Munchausen's. Maybe he could tell Reingold about it, they could write it up and get *that* into the *New England Journal of Medicine.*

But what if he wasn't inventing it? Okay—just what was it he wasn't inventing?

Suppose there *was* a virus causing an epidemic of some kind—then there was little or nothing he could do anyway. There was no cure for viruses, once they were in your body—you had to just let them run their course. They were like perfect little parasites, living inside human cells, unable to survive for very long outside. They pirated the machinery of the organisms they chose as their hosts. Unwanted little guests. A bit like Abel Winston's tapeworm except Jordan had no egg, no cookie, no hammer.

Abel had also said that in medicine, patience was the key. If there *was* an outbreak of something now, should Jordan simply patiently let it run its course? Every epidemic had a natural life span, after all, dependent on population density, environmental conditions, communicability, virulence, mode of transmission. Every virus had a different degree of contagion, for instance—the typical rhinovirus, responsible for the common cold, could infect someone if just one single viral particle got inside the nose; whereas the AIDS virus required *many* particles, transmitted much more intimately, for the disease to spread. And of course some viruses priced themselves out of the market: They were so virulent they killed their host before the unwitting carrier had a chance to pass on the tiny bugs to someone else.

So how could Jordan patiently wait around, if Chessie might be in danger? No, he had to try to stop this (possibly imaginary) epidemic. But how? Isolate the carriers? Chessie had already isolated herself, it seemed. Too late, if she'd already caught something—the only time a virus was vulnerable was before it entered the cells of its host, when it was free-floating, endangered by even the mildest environmental challenges—sunlight, temperature change, any old thing. Failing that, the only way to kill a virus was either to let it run its course—or kill its host.

Jordan finished his drink just as Diana walked up and sat down. Diana, the nurse he'd jilted over the phone two nights before to see Chessie.

"Hey, Jordan Marks the spot. How long you been here, babe?"

Jordan counted his cups. "Let's see . . . three Jack Daniels, one chili, one beer . . ."

"What's that, about ten minutes?"

She was altogether too cheery for his mood, which was by now bleak to sodden. Nonetheless, he tried to smile. "I'm expecting someone." It made him feel like shit to put her off again, but then he already felt like shit.

She had her act together, though, fortunately for them both. "Hey, that's cool," she said, rising. "Maybe next time."

She left, and he ordered another Jack Daniels.

Chessie had spent the morning at Ahab's Basement making calls, then gone home to change—back to Dolores's apartment—which was where Lone Ranger spotted her. He then tailed her to a bar where she met two other women, at which point all three went to a steak and lobster place up the coast.

Ranger was glad for the opportunity to eat. He'd been working such long hours lately he'd neglected himself in that regard, and only now realized how ravenous he was.

He had two filet mignons in a corner booth while the three women carried on at a window table overlooking the sea. Chuffa chuffa chuffa, they did go on. He wondered if he should take all three at once, release them from these earthly chains. No, it was just the *one* he wanted tonight. Chessie.

After a long dinner—during which Ranger had one more scotch than he wanted—the women left again, and again Lone Ranger followed. This time they led him to *another* restaurant—Ports—where they sat at the bar.

Ranger took a table, ordered an espresso. He thought Chessie looked funny at him once, but he was sure she hadn't made him. Just likes the thought of my hard, naked head rubbing up between her legs, he thought, and smiled.

After a while the two other women got up and went back to the bathroom. They were gone maybe five minutes. Chessie lit up a cigarette, inhaled deeply, put it out again, lit another. Ranger almost made his move on Chessie right then, but some other guy moved in on her, so Ranger held back.

She was holding her own with the yahoo at the bar when her girlfriends returned. She used the opportunity to make her own escape to the bathroom, so Mr. Cool got to turn his charms on the girlfriends.

Ranger had a pretty full bladder himself—all those scotches and coffees, no pit stops along the way. He wondered if there was one bathroom back there, or two. Fairly small restaurant; if there was only one, he could maybe wander back there now, maybe kill two birds with one stone, so to speak.

He got up, meandered to the back, down a short hall. Phone, wall mirror, settee. Two bathroom doors. He checked the men's—one toilet, one sink, nobody inside. He stumbled to the women's—if he acted a little drunk, he could laugh it off as a mistake.

80

He looked around to make sure nobody was watching, and opened the door.

Nobody inside.

He backed out fast, looked up at the bar: Her two girlfriends were still there, shaking their heads at the jerk trying to put the make on them, but Chessie was gone.

He looked quickly around the alcove for other rooms she might have gone into. Only one other door here, though—the rear exit. He opened this door and stepped out into the back alley.

Empty. A part of a tire track, a smouldering cigarette stub, some garbage cans, a scaredy cat. No Chessie. She must've known she was being followed, then; known, or suspected. But she couldn't have suspected *him*—this escape had been set up way in advance. Could someone else be after her, then? He looked over his shoulder; he'd have to be more careful. He checked around a minute, then went back inside. When he got back to the bar, the girlfriends were gone, too.

Ranger shook his head in disbelief at himself, how stupid he'd been. He went to the front door, stood outside a minute, but there was no sign of any of them. The maître d' came out momentarily, to make sure Ranger wasn't trying to stiff his bill, but Ranger strolled back to his table, sat down, shook his head again, and ordered another scotch.

He had to give them credit, they played a good game, and he loved a good gamer. Foxed him completely. He'd have to pick up her trail again tomorrow. He admired her though. Whomever she was evading, she was doing it well. So for the moment, he would drink to her prowess, and to the game. The rest of tonight he would make his own.

He went to the bathroom with single-minded purpose, paid his food tab, sat at the bar, ordered another scotch. And one for his friend here.

The jerk thanked Ranger, asked him what he did for a living.

"Demolition," smiled Lone Ranger. "How about yourself?"

"Gimmicks," said the loser. He took out a pack of mentholated slim 100s and a lighter, flicked up a flame, offered one to Ranger, who declined.

"Gimmicks?" said Ranger.

The guy handed his cigarette lighter to Ranger. It was clear plastic, with some kind of two-dimensional diorama inside—a nubile couple, flagrante delicto—and when you tipped the lighter upside down, their clothes fell off. "Stuff like that," the guy chuckled. "Cute for gifts."

Ranger smiled with premonition. "Lighter any good?" he asked, handing it back.

"Oh, yeah," the jerk assured him, clicking the flint twice, producing fire twice. "The product is excellent." He laid it on the bar.

"Reminds me of an old Alfred Hitchcock show," Ranger eased into it, "with Steve McQueen and Peter Lorre. You ever see it? Lorre bets McQueen McQueen's lighter won't light ten times in a row. Bets him a new convertible parked out front against one of McQueen's fingers—Lorre gets to cut off McQueen's finger if McQueen loses. You ever see it?"

The jerk shook his head, smiling uncertainly at a funny look in Ranger's eye.

Ranger picked up the lighter off the bartop, turned it upside down, watched the little fuckers strip, turned it rightside up again, clicked on the flame, and spoke quietly to Mr. Cool-with-the-Ladies. "Care to make a little bet?" he asked.

It was quite late when Jordan reached Dolores's apartment, and he was quite toasted. He rang the bell, no answer. He knocked and knocked. Nobody home. No Dolores, no Chessie. He raised his fist to knock again . . . then stopped, sighed, leaned against the doorframe, closed his eyes, felt the cool wind stir on his cheek, the night-blooming jasmine like a heavy perfume, heard somebody's old Everly Brothers tape playing out a nearby window, the buzz of a worn-out neon light somewhere beyond the corner . . . felt these things, and opened his eyes, but could not know that even in the dim glow of the corner streetlight, his eyes were beginning to look a bit bloodshot.

Part II

LANG

CHAPTER 6

Tuesday morning, December 31, New Year's Eve day, Jordan peered in the mirror and believed his eyes were looking a little red. His first thought was that he was hung over; then, that it was just his recurrent blepharitis—an inflammation of the eyelids and surrounding tissues, which he commonly got from the dry air and pollens of the Santa Anas. Then he remembered noticing that the Santa Anas had stopped yesterday, a memory of the still, windless haze over the observatory. The image arrested him, unsettled him, and he just stared blankly inward a long moment at the yellow chemical smog that surrounded the green domes he'd seen. Like a vision of the apocalypse.

He wondered if his reddening eyes were the early warning signs of the thing he sought. The imaginary epidemic.

He dressed quickly, resolved now to make his case to Hall, clearly and concisely.

So he went to Hall's office, just off the morgue—a macabre little den full of bones and skulls, bottles of floating organs, a large microscope, charts on the walls, books piled high, Victorian surgical instruments on display. As Jordan entered, though, he found Hall talking to another man.

"Oh, I'm sorry, I'll come back . . ."

"Jordan, this is Detective Burns," said Hall. "He's investigating the murder of Billy Lewis."

Burns was just under six feet tall, just under sixty years old. He had graying hair, and the tired eyes of someone who's not only seen it all, but seen it all twice.

"How do you do?" said Jordan, studying the man.

"Not bad, considering," smiled Burns.

"Got any suspects yet?" Jordan tried to sound merely curious.

"Well, the wife is number one, of course." Right to the heart of things.

"Cherchez la femme, right?" Jordan tried to cast Burns the fool. But Burns was nobody's fool.

"Goes a little deeper than that, doc," he explained, more instructive than patronizing. "She was on record as having reported him for wife-beating."

"But hey," Jordan's anger was ill concealed, "that's just a 'domestic beef,' right?"

Burns looked at him coolly. "I understand you were a friend of hers, doctor."

Jordan straightened. "I *am* a friend, yes." He tried to hear accusation in Burns's voice, but there was none; if anything, a kind of fatigue, a sense that Burns hoped it would be simple.

"You have any idea where she might be hiding?" Burns put it directly.

Jordan paused, shook his head, decided to play it close to his chest. "You consider this might be drug-related?" he suggested. "Chessie told me once that he was a coke dealer."

"Could be anything, really, at this point," Burns nodded. He said it with a mask of earnest concern, just the way Jordan spoke to freaked-out family members of a critical patient: It could be anything, ma'am, we'll do our best.

Hall entered the standoff. "Those little prickles in his cheek were cactus needles, Jordan."

"From what?"

Hall shrugged. "Jumped into a cactus bush? Assaulted with cactus? Snorting cactus?" He raised his eyebrows up and down, and whispered, "Death by cactus."

Jordan said, "Are you sure it was murder?"

"What else?"

"What about, in fact, a clinical syndrome of nosebleeds, eyebleeds, and brainbleeds?"

Hall just shook his head. "We've been over this ground already, Jordan, and I just don't see it. We have two patients—Breen, who had hypertension leading to a stroke, and Lewis, whose head jumped onto somebody's knitting needle. So what's the connection, besides they both had brains once, and now they don't?"

"Sounds like you've got a touch of the same problem," Jordan snapped, and left.

"Hey, you coming to the New Year's party tonight?" Hall called after him. But Jordan was gone.

He decided to try to lose himself in his work for a while, let his subconscious assimilate all these conflicting facts and impressions, see if anything rose to the top.

That was his state of mind—sort of vague, on automatic pilot—when he entered Room Three an hour later to see his next patient, whom the chart identified as a Thomas Gilroy, thirty-two year old Caucasian male, vital signs within normal limits. Gilroy sat on the gurney, smiling ingenuously. He looked somehow both older and younger than thirty; his eyes seemed wise, but on the verge of wisecrack. His blond hair was thick, his fingers thin, his smile broad and open. "You must be the local healer," he said.

"I'm Dr. Marks," Jordan said patiently, his mind still half elsewhere. "How can I help you, Mr.—" he looked at the chart—"Gilroy?"

Gilroy beamed like a good old boy, and pointed to his face. "It's my nose, buddy—been bleedin' like stink."

Jordan woke up in a hurry. He pulled the otoscope off its wall hook, screwed a nasal funnel onto the light source. "When did it start?" he asked, trying to keep his voice even.

"Couple days ago," Gilroy shrugged. "You seein' a lot of it down here?"

"Some," Jordan allowed, checking his light. "You been having flu symptoms, too?"

"Not really," Gilroy said quickly. "Could it be serious?"

"I'll have to examine you before I can say." He inserted the light up Gilroy's nose, peering through the lens. "You on medication of any kind?"

"Uh-uh."

Not a sign of blood. He looked carefully up the other nostril, poking as far back as he could.

"Ow!" Gilroy sort of yelped, pulling back.

Jordan regarded him with a mixture of confusion and suspicion. "You don't have a nosebleed," he said. There was a flicker of hesitation, a looking-away, in Gilroy's eye. Jordan pressed. "What's this all about?"

He didn't have to press too hard, it seemed—Gilroy caved in right away, though his tone was reserved at first, and then confidential. "That's what I'd like to know, buddy. See, I think it's about this toxic dump the city covered over last month—I think it's leakin' chlorine or PCB, or some shit, and people in the area startin' to react, they gettin' irritated eyes, and nosebleeds, and some of 'em get asthma"—outrage was mounting in his voice, now—"and *I* think it's a big fuckin' cover-up, and any week now, the lid's gonna blow on this story, and when it does, I'm gonna be there to scoop it up." At this, he broke into a big, triumphant smile and produced his press card. "Thomas Gilroy, Channel Eight Update News Research department."

Jordan's impulse was to applaud, but he restrained himself and only smiled back. "What've you got so far?"

"Not much," Gilroy conceded. "Couple pals with symptoms, they live near the landfill. City tells me the dump met federal guidelines, the owner won't answer my calls, I talk to public health, they give me two numbers—the federal nosebleed hotline, which doesn't know shit; and your number, here. So I call here, the lady at the switchboard says Come on down! So here I am." He grinned his big ingratiating grin again, like a game-show host on Name that Disease!

Jordan actually felt his stomach flutter. At last, he wasn't alone, he wasn't totally crazy, or paranoid, or Munchausen, or psuedo-Munchausen, or simply obsessed with the impending doom heralded by his fortieth birthday. "Maybe we could join forces," he suggested.

"Depends what you got," said Gilroy. Now it was his turn to be suspicious.

Jordan recognized the tone of voice, and was instantly at pains to prove to Gilroy that he was a member of neither the establishment nor the cover-up . . . if that's what it was. He produced a list from his pocket—he'd compiled it from the logbook earlier in the day. "This is

91

a list of all the patients who've come in here the past week with bloodshot eyes or bloody noses." He paused, uncertain of his next leap. "I think some of them may be dead now."

"No shit . . ." Gilroy whispered, excited, almost reverent.

"But they haven't died at this hospital," Jordan explained, "so what we need to do is trace these people— see if any of them have died *elsewhere* the last couple days."

Gilroy grew animated, wriggled on his seat like a boy with a calling bladder. "Buddy, this is Pulitzer territory! This is . . ."

Jordan tried anchoring Gilroy's flight with logistics, though he, too, felt a bit giddy. "If we can't reach these people directly, we'll have to call other hospitals, mortuaries . . ." He tore the list neatly in half, giving Gilroy six names.

Gilroy stared at it, marveling. "This could be like a historic document."

It wasn't just news for Jordan, though; he couldn't stand the thought of Chessie being a footnote on a historic document. "I've got a friend on this list, Gilroy," he warned. "And I worry that she's running out of time."

"Hey!" Gilroy tried to revive the party, "Time is just nature's way of making sure everything doesn't happen at once."

Jordan had nothing to add. Least of all the half-paranoid suspicion that his own bloodshot eyes were dragging him down the neck of the same hourglass. "Meet me here this evening."

"Easy, buddy," Gilroy reassured like a brother, "we'll get it done."

*　　*　　*

The afternoon was quiet and Jordan was able to make lots of phone calls from his office. This was his first:

"This is Dr. Marks, from Bay Cities emergency. Is Mr. Piotter home, please?"

"I'm sorry, Mr. Piotter passed away yesterday. Is there something. . . ?"

Jordan was almost too stunned to answer, but managed to mumble some sympathy and ring off.

It took him eleven more calls—to patients, their private doctors, their doctors' hospitals, the hospitals' emergency rooms and morgues—to locate a second death, but there it was, and Jordan began to tremble. And then an hour later, another patient, not quite dead, but in a neurosurgical intensive care unit morbidly called the Vegetable Garden by the doctors who ran it— not quite dead, but stroked out, cerebral hemorrhage, totally gorked. "Definitely a no code," the nurse told Jordan, "DNR." Do not resuscitate. Squash-rot. Waiting for the credits.

That was three for nine on Jordan's list—and 33 percent seemed statistically significant enough to provoke even Reingold. He called.

"Dr. Reingold's office."

"Yes, is he in?"

"Not at the moment. Can I take your number?"

"This is Dr. Marks. I need to speak with him urgently. Where can I find him?"

She gave him a Glendale address, a warehouse on San Fernando Road. He wrote it down on a scrap of paper, bustled out into the main ER, ran around until he found Jill in the pelvic room, speculum upraised, peering between a pair of straddled knees.

93

"Jill, can you cover for me the rest of the day? It's critical."

She slumped visibly, rested her elbow on one of the stirrups, pointed the ducklike silver speculum. "All right, but you owe me two, now."

"Make it three," he smiled, putting his stethoscope in his jacket pocket and running out.

With the exception of Chessie, women seldom refused him.

Driving through Glendale was like driving through Hollywood in 1930. Small pink or yellow or white wood bungalows, tiny manicured lawns that sported small palms. Jordan thought about moving here whenever he drove through, as if he could live a different kind of life here, simpler, more human.

A mile down San Fernando Road, it turned into a factory district, lots of tracks, stone and quarry places, wholesale lumber depots. Lots of Mexican labor here, too: groups of twenty or thirty men standing on certain corners, just waiting to be hired as unskilled workers by contractors who needed an extra hand here or there, to shovel, to carry, to paint. They stood in clusters of two or three now, crouched on their haunches, leaning on walls, smoking, talking. Waiting patiently.

Mexican gangs loitered at other corners. Or if not actually visible, their *placa* could be seen spray-painted on various walls staking out territories, with gang and members' names: XVIIIth St., Gato, Cowboy, Spider, Lonely, Crazy, Diablo. The local *cholos*. Sometimes you'd see the names X'd out with some other gang's spray paint—a territorial dispute, sometimes an act of war. Jordan remembered the kid he'd seen in the ER a couple days before, with the screwdriver in his arm for "goofin' on someone else's *placa*"—making a spray paint transgression. Strange arsenal, strange times.

He finally found the address Reingold's office had given him, and entered the warehouse by a small side door. What he saw was cheese.

Aisles and aisles of cheese, thousands of crates, wheels, blocks, and packets. A dozen men walked around with clipboards, taking inventory, stamping successive lots with red numbers. Jordan walked toward the back.

The huge bays were open, and forklifts were off-loading trucks at the dock, moving the crates into the warehouse. The sides of the trucks read Quesalinda; the crates said the same.

As Jordan reached the end of the aisle, an off-putting smell settled over him, like baby vomit, or a dead mouse. He wrinkled his nose, began breathing through his mouth. Halfway up the next aisle, he saw Reingold talking to a blue-collar man with a red, blustery face and earlobe creases—the old general practitioner's hallmark sign of high cholesterol heart disease.

Earlobe was talking as Jordan approached. "You don't see this kinda thing happening with *American* cheese," he was muttering to Reingold.

"Now let's not . . ." Reingold was placating, when Jordan interrupted.

"Hi—can I talk to you a minute?"

Reingold looked surprised, but not unpleasantly. "Oh . . . hello. Yes, of course. Excuse me, Mr. Laird."

As he accompanied Reingold to the small, glass-enclosed office at the corner of the warehouse, Jordan said, "Bad earlobe creases. Someone ought to warn him to relax a little, maybe lay off the lasagna."

"Earlobe creases?" Reingold laughed. "That's an old wives' tale."

"Yeah, old wives of dead husbands with earlobe creases."

Reingold scoffed. "No statistically significant correlation between ear configuration of any kind and atherosclerotic cardiovascular disease."

Jordan just smiled, the largesse of the philosopher toward the scientist. "So—what's going on here?"

"Listeriosis epidemic, we traced it finally to this bad Mexican cheese. Contaminated at the factory, it looks like."

They reached the office and entered. It consisted of an old, distressed desk, some metal folding chairs, several telephones, and a couple of file cabinets, atop which sat a ten-inch black and white TV with rabbit ears, turned to an all news station. On one wall was a large map of the county, with several dozen pins stuck in it. And tacked to the map was a sheet of Xerox paper, printed up with a quote from Voltaire: "Doctors pour drugs of which they know little, for disorders of which they know less, into patients of whom they know nothing."

Reingold shut the door behind them, closing out the warehouse sounds and smells. Then he opened a bottle of Air-Wick. "Man, it reeks out there."

"The decay of society."

"*Listeria monocytogenes*, I believe."

"Listen," Jordan approached his subject, "about these nosebleeds I've been seeing . . ."

Reingold raised his hand like a patrician. "First of all, I checked every county on our computer linkup, and none of them shows an increased reporting of epistaxis . . ."

"There *is* an epidemic," Jordan tapped the desk with

his index finger, "and not only that, it's *fatal*. I think it leads to brainbleeds."

"Oh, there's an epidemic of brainbleeds, all right." He pointed to the TV droning on the filing cabinet behind Jordan. Jordan turned around to see a newscaster assuming the look of concern they favor when giving bad local news.

"Once again," the newsreader pursed his lips, "police have released a composite sketch of that new serial killer on the loose. Seven people are reported dead now by the man whose MO is to stick a needle up the base of the victim's skull. No motive has yet been found in this latest grisly spree, although police psychologist Walter Groshy has speculated devil worship may have played a part in the murders. Here with us now is . . ."

Jordan stared at the police sketch of what looked like a demented, bald, light-skinned black man. Then, as the newscaster droned on, Jordan sat down hard on the desk, totally disoriented by this turn of events.

"What," he said, "is *that* all about?"

"Just what it says," Reingold shrugged. "Sounds to me like we've got two things going on—dry air, producing nosebleeds, and a psychotic killer, producing news."

Jordan thought a moment, then shook his head. "Not very parsimonious."

Parsimony, as applied in medicine, referred to frugality of cause when diagnosing a complex of symptoms. For example, if a patient came in complaining of chest pain, nausea, and left arm pain, you might posit that the chest pain was caused by pneumonia, the nausea by flu, and the arm pain by tennis elbow, but this would not be a parsimonious diagnosis. Rather, it's usually more correct to look for the least number of causes for the most number of symptoms. So a likelier diagnosis in this instance would be heart attack—a single entity that could be responsible for all three of the symptoms attributable to that patient. Doctors are taught always to seek the most parsimonious explanation for their observations.

It was an argument that struck Reingold deep to his academic heart. "How, not parsimonious?" he said rather archly.

"I don't know, nosebleeds plus eyebleeds, plus strokes, plus a serial killer who induces brainbleeds . . ."

"You're talking apples and oranges, that's all. And what's this about *eye*bleeds? Last time you were talking *nose*bleeds . . ."

Jordan took out his list. "Look. This is a list of epistaxis and conjunctival hemorrhage patients seen in my emergency room over the past week. The ones I've circled have *died* in the last three days."

Reingold studied the paper, first with wrinkled skepticism, then with increasing curiosity. "There does *appear* to be a relationship, on the face of it. . . ."

"I'm *certain* of it, since this afternoon." Jordan sensed an inroad.

"Doesn't necessarily mean a *causal* relationship, of course. The death rate among the elderly in New York City goes up every time ice cream sales in Hong Kong rise. That doesn't mean buying ice cream in Hong Kong kills old people in New York, it just means it's summertime, and as the heat rises . . ."

"If not a causality, then, there's still a commonality."

"Not even that, necessarily. Just a fluke, maybe. An arbitrary collision of random variables."

"Bleeding is bleeding."

Reingold shrugged. "The Santa Anas kick up, people's

eyes and noses get more irritated; a serial killer kicks up, people's brains get reamed. Maybe the serial killer got crazy from the Santa Anas, maybe that's the common link. Those winds get some people very off balance you know."

"I know," said Jordan without expression, staring directly at Reingold.

Reingold just stared at the paper in his hand. "Were bleeding times checked on any of these people? Prothrombin times, clotting times, platelet counts?"

Jordan smiled hopefully, trying not to appear triumphant. "You'll help me, then?"

Reingold paused, walked to the glass partition separating them from the rest of the warehouse. "Can't do it. I've already got four listeriosis deaths here, the mayor's on my back . . ." He looked at the list again. "What did these patients die *of*, exactly? Cause of death, as reported, I mean."

"Three cerebral hemorrhages, one needled in the brain."

Reingold stared at Mr. Laird, who could be seen in the distance, directing another man where to unload his dolly of cheese. "You know what I love about being an epidemiologist? It's like being a medical detective—you gather clues, you build theories . . . you know how we nailed this cheese culprit?"

Jordan didn't know, and at the moment didn't particularly care. He kept his voice measured and certain. "I think there are roughly six days between first minor bleed and death. I have a dear friend who's over five days into the course of the illness, maybe six, now, and I can't find her."

Reingold regarded him sympathetically. "You want to

help a single person, and all I know about is *populations* of persons."

"Populations are *made* of persons!" Jordan shouted unexpectedly. His frustration level was bubbling over.

Reingold mellowed. "She's a good friend, this person?"

"Imagine your best friend was involved."

Reingold removed his glasses, cleaned them on his shirtsleeve. "I haven't seen my best friend in five years. He's in Madison, and we're both trying to make a name, build a career."

Jordan wasn't too far from that himself. "So take a day off, it's New Year's Eve. Forget 'make a name.' Do a favor instead."

Reingold sniffed the Air-Wick with a distant gaze. "'Is it perfume from a dress/That makes me so digress?'"

"Digress, by all means," Jordan encouraged, uncertain of the reference, though he suspected Eliot again, considering the book of verse he'd noticed earlier on Reingold's desk. "Look, Mark Twain is about as esoteric as I get, but I think he once said, 'There is apparently nothing that cannot happen.' And I'm not positive, but I seem to remember he was referring to this strange outbreak of nosebleeds and strokes . . ."

Reingold held up his hand, signaling Jordan to desist. Then he cleared his throat, put on his glasses and his most pedantic voice. "You want someone to do your legwork? I tell you, flat out, I have no time, and at least two projects of greater interest and import. So forget that. You want some assistance of an academic nature? Okay, here it is." He adjusted his shoulders; a lectern almost appeared before him. "To isolate a cause of collective mortality, you must first document the symptoms, then define the syndrome . . ."

"I've done that," Jordan cut in, taking mental notes.

"Get viral and bacteriologic cultures on everyone *with* symptoms . . ."

"I haven't done that. But . . ."

"And finally, find a patient who doesn't fit the typical pattern. Then, what that patient *does* have in common, *no matter how trivial*, is the thing that links all the patients in the epidemic."

The phone rang. Reingold walked toward it.

Jordan crossed to the door. "Does this make me an official public health commando?"

"Not until you learn the secret handshake."

Jordan opened the door. "Well—thanks for your help."

Reingold picked up the phone, said, "Just a minute" into it, wrote something on a card, and walked over to Jordan. "Here's my home number if you come up with anything."

Jordan took the card. "Thanks. I didn't tell you all the details yet, but there might be a toxic dump involved in all this—I'll let you know."

Reingold walked back to the phone. "And if we *do* publish a paper," he smiled, "I promise to get your name on it. At least in a footnote."

Jordan waved and left. Reingold spoke into the phone. The newscaster on the TV said, "On other fronts, the listeriosis epidemic has claimed two more lives."

Elmore Gray unlocked the bank door for Ms. Vargas, and as she stepped outside, she winked at him. Actually winked. He was too surprised to respond before she walked up the street and around the corner. Winked, by God.

Casually, he ambled over to the personnel file, located Ms. Vargas's telephone number, and copied it down. Then he bade a good night to the few remaining employees and went out the back door to the parking garage. Maybe just give that fine Vargas a call tonight, this cold don't get any worse, he thought, sniffling.

He was parked in the first subbasement, B-6. A few other homegoers passed him down the half-dark aisle, but he was in no hurry. Maybe stop for a beer on the way home, imagine what he would say to Vargas.

He reached his car, an old Dodge Dart. Opened the door, got in, fumbled for his keys, stuck them in the ignition, closed the door, turned the keys, battery low, the engine grunted but it wouldn't turn over. Elmore leaned his head back against the headrest.

Lone Ranger rose up silently out of the rear footwell, directly behind the driver's seat.

Elmore pictured Vargas opening her front door, wearing something comfortable, asking him in.

Lone Ranger wrapped his left arm around the front seat, put his palm to Elmore's forehead, holding the old guard's head back firmly against the rest. There was a small space between the bottom of the headrest and the top of the seat, just enough to expose the back of the driver's neck. Lone Ranger put his needle through that space, on the mark, and rammed it home.

Elmore had no thought of struggle. Just Vargas's face, exploding into orange light. He went tonic, then clonic, then limp.

And his life was over.

Jordan drove next to the Bay Cities Police Department, over on Ocean Avenue. He didn't really expect Burns to be there on New Year's Eve, but he thought someone at the station might be willing to contact him, and Jordan could talk to him over the phone. As it turned out, Burns was standing at the front desk when Jordan entered, having a discussion with the desk man about women.

"Nah, I *like* to date divorced women," Burns was saying.

"Sure, cuz you're divorced too," said the desk man, "so you can relate to each other's problems."

"No way. I like 'em because they know what assholes most men are, so if you just show a little class, they're much more eager to please."

"Yeah, you got a little class, I guess," said the desk man.

Jordan approached the bench. "Sounds kind of cynical about women to me, Detective Burns," he smiled.

"Not at all," Burns was quick to clarify, "it's cynical about men."

"I guess that's inevitable, you spend long enough in a cop shop."

"Yeah, I suppose your view of human nature is much more generous in a doc-in-the-box." Burns smiled against the weight of the world.

Jordan held out his hand, and Burns slapped him five, but couldn't mount much enthusiasm.

"You here to confess?" Burns asked.

"I was just wondering if you'd come up with any leads on the whereabouts of Chessie Lewis."

Burns shook his head, as the desk man went back to his racing form. "Frankly, doc, we've lost interest in her as a suspect. Looks like her husband was done by this shish kebab killer. You probably heard . . ."

"You have a victim profile yet?"

103

Burns shrugged. "Some were men, some women. Four of 'em lived in the same neighborhood—a couple had receipts from the same local stores, they all banked at the same bank, actually, one even *worked* there. Bay City Bank. So we're investigating employees who've been fired, loan applicants who've been turned down, that kind of thing. Why, what's your interest?"

Burns clearly was holding back on some details, as Jordan had done earlier. But Jordan's strategy had shifted somewhat now. He was convinced Chessie was in danger from disease, not from the law; and the more agencies and people he had seeking her out, for whatever reason, the sooner she would be found. So he decided to share his list with Burns.

He pointed to the names he'd circled. "These people have recently died of stroke." He paused for effect. "I wonder if your serial killer may have been involved."

Burns scratched his cheek. "What makes you think so?"

"In my ER, I've seen two deaths in two days—both had nosebleeds, one was needled in the brain. Now here we have *more* nosebleed patients, and *more* deaths . . . maybe we should look for more needles, that's all."

Burns studied the list intently, as if he could perceive more clues in the paper, the writing, the smudges. "Like I said, what's your interest?"

"Like you said—" Jordan thought honesty, in this case, the best policy—"Chessie Lewis is a friend of mine." And he didn't want her being a victim of anything, or anybody, anymore. "A good friend. And she's been having nosebleeds."

"Yeah?" said Burns. "That's interesting. She banked at Bay City, too."

CHAPTER 7

Jordan couldn't remember the last time he'd eaten, so he stopped for a beer and a plate of steamed clams on the Santa Monica Pier, to look at the ocean as he mulled things over.

What was this, still New Year's Eve? It seemed like weeks had gone by since yesterday, he felt a leaden fatigue behind his eyes. Well, he was forty, now; his days were *lang*. Sitting in a booth with a plate glass window that overlooked the entire Pacific, the sun cut flat at the waterline, for just a moment he almost thought he could hear mermaids singing, each to each; but squinting harder at the orange ocean, straining to see them riding seaward on the waves, he realized it was only the sound of the cook scraping grease from the griddle in the kitchen behind the bar. He sipped his unlovely beer.

So all the victims banked at Bay City Bank. Meaning what? Nothing unusual in that pattern to Jordan—they banked at the same bank, shopped at the same stores. So they lived in the same neighborhood. So the serial killer probably lives there, too.

So Chessie lives there, too—at least, she *did* live there, when she was still living with Billy. Now she lived . . . nowhere. Not with Dolores anymore, it seemed, either.

Same bank, same stores. Same hospital. Billy had been brought in to Bay Cities ER from right near his home. So the victims used Bay Cities Hospital, too. So?

So he had to find Chessie. Had to find her urgently. He felt chaotic inside, approaching panic—as if he were playing a complicated life-or-death game with an unknown number of players, and everyone knew the rules but him. He was uncertain and afraid, for himself and for Chessie, and all he knew was that if he could just find her, it would all work out, they could figure it out together. Make each other well.

Jordan lingered, in a sort of fugue state, until kitchen voices woke him, and he drowned these nonproductive musings with the last of his beer, sniffled, rubbed his eyes, which felt as if they were full of sand, and left the table without finishing the clams—their texture was suddenly too fleshy.

Ranger kneaded the fleshy pad at the ball of his left thumb as he listened to Dolores sing. Not bad. He liked this thirties stuff, reminded him of old movies on the tube. That's what Dolores reminded him of, too, Jean Arthur or somebody like that. He hoped she'd tell him where Chessie was, right off, avoid a lot of trouble.

When the song was over, Ranger clapped long enough to catch her eye, and then gave her a thumbs-up when he did. She came by his table about ten minutes later.

"Buy you a drink?" he said.

"No, I can't while I'm working. Thanks for the applause, though."

"Voice like that, you oughta get yourself discovered."

"Yeah, just me and everyone else in this town."

"Truth-time, girl. I've had people play their demo

tapes for me while they were driving me in a taxi to the airport."

Her smile tried to capture a certain casualness. "You in the music business?"

"Used to be. Film, now. I heard a voice like yours, I was still in recording, I'd have snapped you up." He snapped his fingers. "Like that."

"Hey, I act, too," she laughed, making it sound like a joke, but for real.

"Yeah? You got a composite or somethin' you could show me, case there's an opening. . . ?"

"Let me guess," she said drily, "you've got a part coming up for me, and the opening is between my legs."

"No, no, I'm on the level, really, just an eight by ten glossy."

She hesitated. Maybe he *was* for real. Producers went to restaurants, too, after all, there was no need to insult the man. "Well, I don't have anything with me. I could just run back to the apartment on my break, though . . ."

"I'll come with you—I'm late as it is, it'll save me some time."

She slouched on one foot, half deflated. "Forget it."

He held up his hands. "Okay, I'll wait here, then. But like I said, I'm running late. If you can make it back in"—he looked at his watch—"ten minutes, I'll take your picture and resumé. If not . . ." He shrugged as if to say it was up to her.

"Deal," she said. She told the manager she was taking ten, and ran out the back to trot home.

Lone Ranger waited one minute, then dropped a five on the table and walked out the front, turning left, toward Dolores's block. Maybe he'd get lucky, and Chessie would be there now.

If not, Dolores would be bound to have something to say on the subject.

Jordan drove down to Redondo as clouds blew in rapidly over the darkening sky, and the wind picked up along the coast. He parked his car a stone's throw from the wharf, and was about to walk down to the dive shop when he noticed Dave, the manager, loading up a big charter boat at the nearest pier.

Jordan grabbed his leather jacket out of the back seat and put it on as he strolled over dockside. The whole area looked deserted, except for Dave. The only sounds were the rising wind in the sheets and rigging on some of the taller masts, water slapping hulls, hulls clunking docks, and three jetties down, laughter and music from a pleasure cruiser whose party was already under weigh.

The name on the stern of Dave's boat was *Ahab's Ride*. Dave was just jumping onto the pilings from it, empty-handed, when Jordan reached him, smiling.

"Hi—remember me?"

"Sure," said Dave, brushing off his hands. "Chessie's friend. How you doin'?"

"Not bad. You got a charter?"

Dave nodded. "Fella wants to go night-trawling."

"Yeah, that's what *I'm* up to."

"How do you mean?"

"Well, I'm looking for Chessie, actually. She been around?"

"No, but she sure has been popular."

"Yeah? Who else is asking?"

"Let's see, there was the cops, and then her friend Dolores, and then old Baldy . . ."

"Who's that?"

"Some guy, he's been here before—wants her to show him the Catalina Reef."

"What's he like?" Jordan asked. Maybe it was irrelevant, just one of her clients. In diagnosis, however, the history was all-important—extract every detail, evaluate its weight later.

Dave smiled at his image of Baldy. "Telly Savalas," he said.

The wind rose again, making the taut lines hum a kind of low-frequency breathy drone, somber, unstructured.

Jordan looked at the sky. "Bad night to be on the water. If it were me, anyway."

Dave reached into his shirt pocket, pulled out a small bottle. "Dramamine," he smiled.

Jordan shivered at the thought of so much pitch and yaw, and handed Dave one of his business cards. "Call me if she shows, okay?"

He used a pay phone at the gas station on the corner to call his answering machine at home. Maybe Chessie had called in.

Chessie hadn't. But Gilroy had. He'd left a message asking Jordan to meet him at the newsroom as soon as possible.

The Channel Eight studio was fairly far down on Sunset, at the east end of Hollywood, almost to Silverlake. Jordan wasn't sure how far, though, so he got off the freeway early, and drove several miles down the boulevard.

Even inland it was chilly now, and dark with the look of rain. Christmas decorations blew wildly from the streetlamps; celebrants blew wildly on their horns, milling on the sidewalks, revving up for midnight. Hookers were out in force, all along Sunset from Highland to Serrano, looking to get warm. How lonely was that, turning tricks on the turning year, Jordan wondered.

Just past the intersection of Sunset and Hollywood, Jordan found Channel Eight. The guard at the front gate waved him into the nearly empty parking lot from the open window of his kiosk. "You must be one o' them whatchamacallits," he shouted at Jordan with curiosity. "One o' them overachievers."

The guard inside the building looked up Gilroy's name and directed Jordan to the second floor, 234, the newswriters' room.

Looked like a lot of activity way down at the end of the hall, full of voices and clatter; but the rest of the building seemed empty. When Jordan pushed the elevator button, both doors opened immediately.

Upstairs, he found Gilroy without problem at the end of a large room filled with two rows of metal desks, a computer screen and keyboard and a telephone atop each one. There was only one other person in the room, a thirty-year-old woman wearing a cardigan and a frown, typing away on her word processor, off in her own universe.

Jordan sat in the chair of the desk adjacent to Gilroy's. "Been here long?"

Gilroy shrugged good-naturedly. "Like the frog said, time's fun when you're having flies."

Jordan held out his hands, palms up. "You got something?"

"Good news and bad, buddy," smiled the newsman.

"Bad first." Jordan braced himself.

"None of the nosebleed patients on the list you gave me have died."

Jordan waited for the hammer to fall but that was it. "Nobody's died, that's bad news? You got a funny idea of bad news . . ."

"Hey, we on the same case, or what?" Gilroy sounded affronted.

It was true, they were looking for connections, and more deaths would have meant more connections; but if nobody else had died, Jordan would not have complained. "So what's going on here?" he said, looking around. The place had a humanless air about it. A two-foot scrawny Christmas tree leaned in the trash can by the door.

"Gotta wait by the phone a while yet," said Gilroy. "Couple more calls left to come in."

"Okay, so what's the good news?"

His face became animated again. "That CDC nosebleed hotline mentioned a similar outbreak in Florida, which translates Miami to me. So I called a friend in vice, guy owes me a major favor over a story I suppressed a couple years ago at the Wadsworth VA . . ."

"Get to the point," Jordan said with stony restraint. This guy was entirely too garrulous for Jordan's mood.

"The point is," said Gilroy, "there's a bad load of coke in the pipeline, cut with some shit makes nosebleeds a lot worse—ta-da!—so by following the trail of dribbling blood, the Feds are tryin' to trace the source of the blow."

Jordan sucked on his lower lip, trying to put everything together. "Jesus, maybe this serial killer is a drug-related thing, then . . ."

"What's the serial killer got to do with . . . ," Gilroy interrupted, confused.

"Like maybe money from the coke deals is in the bank that all the victims used."

111

"What bank? Now what victims we *talkin'* about, here?"

Jordan nodded to his own conclusions. "Billy Lewis was a dealer. You think they're killing anyone who can finger the main source?"

"Who's Billy Lewis?"

Jordan stood up, realizing he'd never really looked at the medical charts of most of the ER epistaxis patients. Of course he'd never had anything specific to look *for* until now; but now he was suddenly wondering if there might not be connections to drug use suggested in some of them—either as a piece of medical history or some physical note.

"Where you goin'?" said Gilroy.

"Hospital. Going to pull the medical records on all these people. Look, can you follow up on this drug deal thing tonight?"

"Yeah, like I said, I'm waitin' for a call. And then I know a couple pushers might tell me somethin'."

"Great—here, meet me at this address at midnight." He wrote down Dolores's address on a piece of paper. "Hopefully, someone will be there by then. If not, we'll just have to break in."

Gilroy regarded him as if from a suddenly new perspective, and was impressed. "Hey, you're one radical dude, buddy."

"Yeah," he almost smiled on his way out, "I'm one of those whatchamacallits."

He drove straight to the ER and gave his list of epistaxis patients to Barb, the night clerk at the front desk. The ER was ghostly quiet now, wouldn't get wild until two or three A.M., when the bars closed and the parties shut down.

"Barb, call these charts down from medical records for me, will you?"

Technically, it was unlawful for Jordan to examine the medical records of a patient not currently in the hospital, if that patient was not under his personal care. But Jordan was a good pal of Barb's, he wrote her prescriptions for her sinusitis all the time; and furthermore, the law didn't make much sense, and people called down random charts from time to time for various reasons anyway; and besides, it was totally quiet down here now, with nothing to do but the crossword puzzle.

So she said, "Sure," and picked up the phone to call medical records.

The Venice boardwalk at Muscle Beach, by nine-thirty, was a street carnival extraordinaire. Colored lights, neon signs, sparklers, and paper lanterns illuminated a milling crowd of roller skaters, burly bikers, surfers, winos, skateboarders, punk-rockers, street musicians, mimes, pot-smokers, body builders, and nightlifers of all kinds. There was a guitar-playing, white-turbaned Sikh on roller skates; there was a short guy telling jokes as he juggled chainsaws; there were pirate fireworks already going off all over the beach: bottle rockets, cherry bombs, M-eighties.

Gilroy walked slowly through the horseplay, looking at addresses on the apartments that fronted the boardwalk until he found the one he wanted. It was where a certain pusher was now living—that's the call Gilroy'd been waiting for, learning this guy's current digs. Be lucky to find him home tonight, but who knew. Maybe the party was at *his* place tonight.

Gilroy walked down an alley, knocked on the third

door in. Twisted Sister was blasting away on the stereo inside. Gilroy knocked louder.

The music was turned down, footsteps approached the door. A voice on the other side called out, "Who is it?"

"Tommy Gilroy, buddy. Lookin' for Crack-man."

The door opened four inches, stopped by six chains, set from top to bottom. A shadowy face peered out at Gilroy. A longhair, wearing three earrings shaped like bells in one ear, a rhinestone stud in his nose. And one bloodshot eye.

"What for?" said Longhair.

Gilroy grinned like Santa Claus and held up a twenty dollar bill. "Just wanna buy a little information, buddy."

Jordan sat at the cluttered desk of the doctors' office behind the ER with a stack of medical charts before him, some thin, some thick, some two-volume sets. He pulled down the top chart, opened it to the first page.

Conrad Cheremoya.

"Cheremoya, Cheremoya . . . ," Jordan said out loud, trying to remember where he'd heard the name. He looked at the man's most recent ER sheet, and read the history: *This 72-year-old Caucasian male brought in by paramedics with chief complaint of massive nasal bleeding X 2 hours. Blood pressure in the field 70/40, no previous history, on no meds . . .*

Right, Jordan remembered now, this was the patient just being transferred up to the operating room as Jordan was coming in for work Saturday. Jerry Hoffman had seen the guy that night, couldn't stop the bleeding, and sent him upstairs.

Seventy-two years old. Seemed unlikely the guy had been doing any cocaine. Jordan scanned the physical exam, then went through Cheremoya's course in the hospital. A short one, it turned out: successful minor surgery, a couple days without event, his pressure came up to normal with some IV fluids, the nasal packs were pulled out, and he was discharged. Sent home today, doing well.

Jordan tapped his fingers on the discharge diagnosis, trying to hear the mermaids over the noise of the spattering grease. *Anterior nasal hemorrhage. Doing well. Return to clinic in two days for follow-up.*

The phone rang out front in the ER. Jordan put Cheremoya's chart aside, and took down the next one from the top of the pile. Before he could open it, though, Barb called to him from the front desk.

"Jordan, there's a Detective Burns on line two . . ."

"Thanks," Jordan answered, ·punched the button for line two, and picked up his phone. "Lieutenant—what's up?"

"New Year's Eve, you know, it's not so easy to track down information."

"But?"

"But I'm a dedicated law enforcement officer, and I'm here working because I got Christmas off, and if I'm working tonight, why shouldn't somebody else do a little work too, you know what I mean?"

"So you got some information you want to share?"

"Yeah, I'm a sharing kind of guy. Besides, since you're so interested, I thought if I gave you a little feedback, you might check a few things for me that you had easier access to than I do. You know, medical stuff."

"Okay . . . so?"

"So those names you gave me, the dead nosebleeds? I checked with the coroner's office, a few mortuaries, some other places. One corpse was cremated, two buried

115

without autopsies, two *did* have autopsies, one was a coroner's case . . . and guess what—they both had bleeding in the brain, even though cause of death on one was listed as myocardial infarction—what's that, a heart attack?"

"Yeah, heart attack, wouldn't cause cerebral bleeding at all. What did the autopsies say the bleeding was caused by?"

"One said aneurysm, one just speculated the patient hit his head when he fell after the supposed heart attack. But you know what's weird? Most of 'em banked at Bay City. Just like the murder victims."

"Most of them banked at Bay City . . . ," Jordan repeated.

"Yeah. Let's see . . . all of 'em except . . . Breen. Guy named Dennis Breen. He was the only one banked somewhere else."

"Breen." Jordan squinted, rubbed his eyes.

"Yeah. So what I'd like *you* to do is get the medical records of these people together, and tomorrow or whenever, I'll come by and the two of us can go over them together, maybe we can find some *other* similarities that would be helpful."

"That's not exactly . . . legal, is it?"

"Hey, I could subpoena every record, and subpoena you, too, but I don't see any point in that. So get real. If we find anything that looks promising, I *will* subpoena the charts—this is just a little less paperwork, makes it easier on everybody."

"No problem," said Jordan. His only problem was he had to find Chessie tonight. He *had* to. He was about to tell Burns about the drug angle, but Burns spoke first.

"Terrific—so I'm off now, so I'll see you in the morning, but not too early, I got a great party I'm off to now."

"Right. Well . . . okay, thanks, lieutenant. Have a good time. Happy New Year."

"Yeah, you too, doc. See you next year." He cleared some phlegm and hung up.

Jordan put back the receiver, went through the stack of charts one more time, and came up with Breen's.

The atypical patient. That's what Reingold had said. Find the patient who's different from all the others, and what that patient had in *common* with all the others, *no matter how trivial*, was the thing that linked them in the epidemic.

And Breen had banked at a different bank from the others who had died. Financial atypia.

Jordan ran his finger slowly down Breen's ER sheet, examining every word, every detail: name, address, date, time of arrival, phone number, date of birth, mother's maiden name, hospital number, insurance carrier . . .

Now *there* was something minimally eye-catching. Typically, patients were covered by one of a half dozen common medical insurance policies: Blue Cross, Medicare, SAG, CNA, Prudential, Maxi-Care, Cash, Medi-Cal. This one was different. This third-party coverage was issued by CHAMPUS. Jordan had seen this designation a couple times a year, at most; but now it rang a bell. The clerk would know, this was her domain.

"Barb," he called out, "what's CHAMPUS insurance?"

She yelled back, "Government, like civilian but military coverage, I think—you know, like FBI, CIA, military dependents, that kind of thing."

At which moment, serendipity struck. For as Jordan was staring blankly down at the desk, head tilted toward the open door so he could hear Barb better, his gaze came to focus on the corner of a manila envelope buried under all the rubble of the desk; an envelope with Dennis Breen's name scribbled on it in Jordan's handwriting. The envelope with Breen's personal effects in it, hidden there inadvertently since Breen's death, when Jordan had dislodged the contents of half a shelf on top of it in his haste to deal with some now-forgotten crisis in the ER. Personal effects sought by Breen's family for the past day and a half, in fact—only to be told by the nurses they spoke to that nobody could yet find the items in question, but certainly they would turn up.

So now they turned up. Jordan extracted the envelope from the mess, gently closed the door to his office, opened the envelope, cleared a space on his desk, and emptied the contents out to view.

The first thing to strike his eye was a blank deposit slip from the Bay City bank. Blank, but not quite unused: on its back were a series of geometric doodles done in ballpoint pen.

So Breen hadn't banked at Bay City; yet he *had*.

The second item of interest was a computer printout codenamed ECHO-121. And the printout contained a listing, of all things, of the access codes to what appeared to be all the hospital billing computers in the county.

There was a floppy disk encased in a plain, white envelope.

There was Jordan's unfilled prescription for Breen's antihypertensive medication.

There was a billfold with credit cards, driver's license, insurance cards, a bank card—Bank of America—an auto club card, eighty-three dollars . . . but no names, numbers, pictures, business cards. Nothing personal at all, except the one emergency phone number Jordan had called. The people who'd claimed the body.

There was a clip-on, laminated, photo ID badge with Breen's name and picture, from a company called Genenco.

And there were five keys on a ring.

Jordan picked up the deposit slip again. "But he didn't bank here," he muttered.

Jordan examined the printout more carefully. In the upper left-hand margin were the words USERNAME: ECHOVECTOR. This was followed by an alphabetical list of 117 hospitals, each one attached to an access code. Jordan found Bay Cities Hospital on the list, with its own code. He flipped on his desk terminal, punched in the hospital username, BAYCIT, punched in his personal password, ROMEO, brought up the menu . . . and then punched in the access code listed on Breen's printout.

There was a ten-second delay—blank screen, like an unfocused eye, as the computer was thinking—and then the screen lit up with a long display of all the patients who'd come through the hospital in the month of December. They were listed alphabetically, with billing information, date of admission, date of discharge, and discharge diagnosis. You could bring up any patient desired, up to ten at a time on the screen.

Why would Breen want all this? For every hospital in town?

Jordan cleared the screen and inserted Breen's floppy disk into the computer. It was incompatible, though. All that lit up was DOES NOT COMPUTE.

He removed the disk, put it down, picked up the ID badge. Breen's name and photostat—a terrible Polaroid likeness—were positioned above the name and address of the company. Genenco, 2217 Lincoln Blvd., Bay City, California.

119

Genenco. A genetic engineering firm, Jordan thought, he wasn't sure—but that wasn't the tug of recognition he was feeling. It was something else. He opened his top left drawer and pulled a leaf of Bay Cities Hospital stationery out. The address at the top of the page was 2524 Lincoln Blvd., Bay City, California.

Genenco was just three blocks away.

Like the bank, the hospital, the stores, Genenco was another neighborhood place.

The serial killer's neighborhood.

Jordan flipped through Breen's hospital chart—just a few pages thick—to the death certificate. Cause of death was written in as cerebrovascular accident. Jordan looked to the bottom of the page, to see who'd signed it: Dr. William Harris.

Jordan turned to the next page, the autopsy form. It was blank, except for the red, rubber-stamped letters WAIVED. Jordan looked to the bottom of the page, to see who'd authorized the waiver. Again, Dr. William Harris, this time with his name printed beneath the signature, and a phone number penned in beneath that.

So who the hell was this Harris? Maybe *he* had some clearer idea of what was going on, some bit of data or insight into Breen's death.

Jordan picked up the phone and push-buttoned the number printed under Harris's name on the autopsy waiver. The phone rang four times before being answered. It was a woman's voice, cool and nasal:

"Good evening—Genenco. May I help you?"

CHAPTER 8

Jordan was so taken aback, he didn't respond for a moment. "Yes . . . hello . . . is Dr. Harris in?"

"Nobody is in at the moment, but business hours will resume on January second. This is the answering service. Would you care to leave a message?"

"No . . . no . . . thank you." Jordan was too confused to think on his feet. "I'll call back in the morning."

"Normal business hours will resume on . . ."

But Jordan hung up on her courteous advisory.

His pulse was quickening; but what did he have? Dennis Breen, the atypical victim; Genenco, a local firm that printed out patient profiles on its computer; patients, dying of cerebral hemorrhage—by disease or misadventure; a batch of killer coke; a floppy disk.

He came back to the floppy disk. It would be nice to read it. It connected Breen, Genenco, the neighborhood, patients, the mysterious Dr. Harris.

He could turn this stuff over to the cops, but what would happen? Days of decision, paperwork, subpoenas—plenty of time for evidence to be hidden or destroyed by anyone interested. Way too much time, if Chessie was really in danger. But in danger from what? Serial killer? An epidemic generated by a mad scientist from Genenco? Monster cocaine? Was that what Breen was, an FBI agent on a big coke bust?

Jordan increasingly felt that he not only had to know, he had to know tonight. Last night he was forty years old; tomorrow night, for all he knew, he might be dead. Tonight, he had to be with Chessie. And tonight, he had to know.

He called Burns back at the station, but Burns was already gone, and not reachable until morning. "Definitely not reachable," said the desk man.

Jordan wasn't deterred, though. If anything, he was buoyed by a rush of nervous energy. He went through his jacket pockets, found Reingold's card with the home phone scribbled on the back, and called. Reingold answered after one ring.

"Reingold here."

"Art? Jordan Marks. How you doing?"

"Pretty good, just watching an old movie, here, I've seen it before, though. What are you up to?"

"Listen, something's developed, I want you to meet me at the diner on the corner of Twenty-second and Wilshire."

"Sure, you want to do breakfast?"

"No, right now, it's urgent."

"Now? What time is it?"

"Eleven-fifteen. You don't come now, you'll miss the party."

"Not a wine and *cheese* party, I hope." His smile was almost audible over the phone.

"Forget your damn fermented cheese," Jordan smiled back. "We've got fermented *brains* to fry." He was mixing his metaphors in a parody of high drama; but he didn't realize how prophetic he was being.

"Brains to fry," Reingold echoed. "Isn't that sweet-breads?"

"No, sweetbreads is pancreas. I don't know if the diner has any this late, though."

"I'll be there in half an hour, maybe we'll get some leftovers."

Jordan hefted the floppy disk. "Don't worry, we'll pick over the menu."

Jordan sat in the Bay Café at a booth facing the door, sipping coffee. The clock showed fifteen minutes to 1986, but the other patrons in the small, all-night diner seemingly couldn't have cared less. There was a young derelict in torn shoes, torn pants, torn life; a couple of pimps; an insomniac-looking woman wearing hospital slippers; a few teens between parties; an angry, older man, continuously talking to himself. Café of the Walking Wounded.

Reingold entered, dressed in khaki pants, running shoes, an old Levi shirt, and a pullover. He walked straight to Jordan's booth, sat down, looked at him wordlessly, then leaned across the table and pulled down Jordan's lower eyelid, exposing the increasingly red white.

"What's the matter with your eye?" he demanded. Doctorial reflex.

"That's maybe what we're here to find out."

"Looks like a little seborrheic blepharitis, to me. Some conjunctivitis. Hydrocortisone ointment, twice a day, should do you nicely."

"Yeah, I do that. I think I'm afraid—I mean, I'm ex-cited, but afraid, you know what I mean? Like I'm on to

123

something, and it's very clever of me, but the answer isn't real desirable . . ."

"I don't follow you."

"I mean I'm sure it's partly because I just turned forty, and I'm confronting the fact of my mortality, and all that shit, but partly it's this case, and then meeting Chessie again, too . . ."

"You're forty? Gee, you don't look forty."

The waitress appeared, and appeared depressed. Reingold looked up at her. "You think he looks forty?" he said, nodding toward Jordan.

She looked at Jordan half-heartedly, ignored the question, took out her pad and pen. "You want coffee too?" No schmoozing tonight. Tonight *everyone* was a year older.

"Tea for me, please," Reingold refused to be glum, even flanked by this manic-depressive duo. The waitress left in a snit, and Reingold gave Jordan a comradely smile. "So—'waddaya know, waddaya say?' That's from an old film."

Jordan hunkered down. "This is what I know: Some people getting nose- or eyebleeds are dying or being killed about six days later. It seems to be connected with a bad shipment of cocaine. And maybe with this . . ."

He removed Breen's floppy disk from his jacket pocket.

Reingold picked it up, took it out of its white, square sleeve, looked at it. "Looks like a floppy disk."

Jordan then took the printout from his pocket and pointed to the words USERNAME: ECHOVECTOR at the top left of the page. "Can you run the program?" he said.

Reingold shrugged. "I could bring up the menu with

one cerebral hemisphere tied behind me. Which items on the menu I had *access* to would depend on a personal password." He put the disk back in its envelope, then slipped that into his pocket. "I'll take it to the office in the morning, though, run it through my system, see what I come up with . . ."

"Won't wait," Jordan shook his head. "And it's not compatible with the hospital computer—I think we have to use the machine it was programmed on."

Reingold looked around skeptically. "What—here at the diner?"

"Across the street."

Reingold peered across the street. It was a squat, concrete, two-story building, its windows all darkened, one light on in the front foyer. The small title on the front door was barely visible.

"Genenco," said Reingold flatly. "They're a genetic engineering firm."

"I believe so." Jordan kept his smile thin, to contain himself.

"You want to go over *there* and run this program?"

"Right now."

"It's the middle of the night."

"The night is young."

"You think they'll let us just walk in?"

"We'll have to sneak in," Jordan said.

"Forget it. That's breaking and entering."

"Not exactly, I don't think." He took out Breen's keys and ID badge, laid them on the table. "We'll just use Breen's keys to get in, and Breen's ID if there's a security guard. I'll just say he loaned them to me, told me to use his office whenever I . . ."

Reingold interrupted with traces of annoyance, fear,

and curiosity all mixed in. "And just who the hell is Breen?"

"Breen, I believe, is the dead government agent whose floppy disk knows all about this epidemic."

"This epidemic of nosebleeds."

"And brainbleeds. And I wouldn't be surprised if an echovirus turned out to be involved."

"I've never heard of an echovirus that produces nosebleeds . . ."

Jordan pointed to the title of the printout. "What about ECHO-121?"

"Nor have I ever heard of a fatal echovirus—nor a curable one, for all of that. I mean if you *do* have a case of something, or your friend does, there's nothing to be done—your body will generate an immune response and overpower the little buggers, or it won't."

"And what about *public* health? What about preventing this disease from spreading through the community? That doesn't concern you?"

"Of *course* it concerns me! I just don't know what disease you're talking about." He looked baffled. "You've talked about toxic dumpsite leaks, you've talked about bad cocaine shipments . . ."

Jordan's mind was leaping ahead. "I wonder if some big cocaine cartel launders their money through Genenco. Or maybe Genenco is actually secretly *funded* with drug money. How's this—a hundred kilos of coke sitting in the Genenco basement, waiting for distribution, got contaminated with . . ."

Reingold was irate. "I absolutely refuse to let you go on with this flight of ideas."

"Look, I've got to find out tonight if this is a cocaine thing or not, because if it is, I can stop worrying about Chessie so much, because she doesn't use it." He locked

126

Reingold's eyes with his own, tried to pull him in with emotion, since logic wasn't quite working. "I mean, I need to find her tonight anyway, but I want to be able to tell her she's safe, safe with me, and she's not going to die, and neither am I."

"You're not going to die . . ." Reingold tried his doctor-reassurance voice, but it wouldn't work on another doctor.

"Look at this eye," Jordan whispered fiercely, pulling down his lower lid. "Conjunctival irritation. *You're* the one who told *me* echovirus could cause conjunctival irritation. *You're* the one who asked *me* what was wrong with my eye. There's echo on this printout, and maybe on that floppy disk, and maybe in cocaine all over the city, and God knows where, and you're worried about running a computer program, nobody's even going to know, in the middle of the night . . ."

"The night is young," Reingold said gently.

Jordan stopped, smiled. "Look, with or without you, I'm going. I'd just like some independent verification of what I find out."

Reingold was turning, almost pleading now. "I could lose my job if we're caught."

"You could also break open a great case. What were your words—'gathering clues . . . nailing culprits . . .'"

Reingold looked at Breen's badge. "I've got no ID like you. What if there *is* a guard?"

"Use your Public Health Service ID—we'll say you're auditing the facility, if anyone asks. Just act like you belong there, for Chrissake, and people *believe* you belong. Works every time. Anyway, doctors never get arrested, not so it sticks."

"Arrested, I'm not so worried about. My *career*, I'm worried . . ."

127

"Look, now or even later, we'll just say I told you I was Breen, you had no reason to question it, and I asked you to come to my office to check some data I was concerned about for public health reasons, and I asked you to come at night so as not to arouse alarm."

Reingold looked helplessly around the diner, as if someone might explain away this madman to him. "This is totally unacceptable. . . ."

"Art, come on, what else you doing tonight? It's New Year's for God's sake, do something new. Hey, I saw those movie posters on your wall—*The Maltese Falcon, The Third Man, The Thin Man* . . ."

"Those are *movies*."

"You'll never get another chance like this."

Outside, explosions thudded in the distance, like the climax of a final battle, the new year pounding down the army of the old. On the wall, the clock read 11:56, but in here nobody seemed to notice. The Restaurant that Time Forgot.

"Someone like me doesn't do things like this," Reingold tried to explain.

The waitress returned, set a cup down in front of Reingold. Not tea, but coffee.

"This isn't what I ordered . . . ," Reingold began, but the waitress was already gone.

"Don't some things just plain piss you off?" said Jordan.

Fifteen minutes later they were standing at the front door of Genenco, Inc., shivering in their shoes. Reingold scanned the street, jittery as a junkie trying to score, while Jordan affixed Breen's clip-on ID to his lapel.

"Come on, come on," whispered Art.

Jordan began sticking various keys from Breen's ring in the lock. He tried all five, and none of them worked. "Shit."

"Let's get out of here," said Reingold.

Jordan tried the keys again, and this time the second one worked. "Just had to jiggle it," he said. Softly, they entered, as he whispered, "Remember, anybody asks, you're with me."

They'd hardly gone three steps before an unseen voice accosted them. "Can I help you gentlemen?"

Just beyond the corner they were passing sat a security guard at a reception desk not visible from the street. The guard was holding a paperback, and looked to Jordan to be more interested in the next page than in the intruders before him.

So after the momentary alarm, Jordan strode forward with his usual air of authority, leaving Reingold a couple paces behind, and smiled like an employer at the guard. "Hi. Left something in my desk."

The guard was already back to his book, though, as soon as he visualized the general shape of the correct ID badge on Jordan's shirt. Face down, eyes moving, he waved them in. Jordan motioned Reingold, and led him, without another word, through the double doors that fronted the first-floor corridor.

They walked slowly past door after door. Jordan felt focused; Reingold looked stunned.

"I can't believe we're in here," he said.

"I can't believe it was so easy," said Jordan, though in some funny way, acting so brazenly, as if he *did* belong here, made him in fact *feel* like he belonged here. His stride changed quickly from tentative to bold.

Each door they passed had a title on it: Laminar Flow

Room, Hyperbaric Chamber, Culture Incubation, Enteric Lab, Isotope Storage, Library, Dr. J. Murnane, Dr. A. Rechtschaffen, Dr. D. Madansky . . . and at the end of the hall, the last door on the right, Dr. D. Breen.

Jordan tried the knob, but it was locked. He went back to the key ring, and the fourth one worked. He opened the door. Cleaned out. Totally empty. The office now dead as the man.

"Ring out the old, ring in the new," said Jordan, easing back into the hall.

"So the computer's gone, too," Reingold urged in a low voice, "so let's us be gone."

Jordan walked back down the hall, trying every door. When he reached the office of Dr. P. Calabra, the door yielded to his pressure, and he entered. Reingold followed.

It was a small office, overflowing with books, journals, reprints. And there was a computer terminal on the desk.

"Voilà," said Jordan, sitting down at the desk.

There was a desk speakerphone beside the terminal, an open book on polymerases beside that, and beside that a Tinkertoy model of a DNA molecule. On the bulletin board behind him was tacked a mélange of memos, scribbled equations, bibliography references, *New Yorker* cartoons, and a hand-printed sign that read, in large, block-letters: We Sell Designer Genes. And in smaller print, below that: Alterations While-U-Wait.

"Let me have the disk," said Jordan. Reingold reached into his pocket and handed it over. Jordan slipped it into the slot and turned on the machine as Reingold walked around to stand behind him.

The screen lit up with a series of numbers and letters, bright green on dark gray.

"They ought to switch to amber," Reingold noted. "It's easier on the eyes."

The screen went blank for several seconds, then flashed the words ECHO-121 three times, then went blank again, then printed up a single word.

USERNAME:

"This is pointless," said Reingold, "we still don't have any kind of personal password."

After the word USERNAME, Jordan punched in the word ECHOVECTOR. The screen went blank again, briefly, then came up with a short but tantalizing format.

```
ECHOVECTOR PROJECT MENU
1. FUNDING
2. GENETICS
3. COMPLICATIONS
   A. MEDICAL
      i. PATHOPHYSIOLOGY
      ii. EPIDEMIOLOGY
         I. CASE RETRIEVAL
         II. CARTOGRAPHICS
   B. POLITICAL
4. PROGRAM—ADA
   A. QUERY
   B. INPUT
```

"Intriguing menu," said Jordan. "Would you agree?"

Reingold remained silent, reading the screen. Jordan punched number 1.

The screen went blank, then flashed the words ACCESS DENIED.

"Told you so," said Reingold.

Jordan punched 2, 3A, 3B, and 4A. All denied access. 4B got him one step further, though. The screen cleared, and came up with a single command.

PASSWORD:

Jordan typed in GENENCO.
Access denied.
He typed in BREEN.
Access denied.
"ADA," Jordan said, straining his memory. "You know anything about that program? It's government, isn't it?"

Reingold nodded. "Department of Defense. Public Health uses it a little, mostly in overlap areas."

"So what's ADA an acronym for? American Defense something?"

Reingold smiled. "It's not an acronym. It's a person's name. Ada Lovelace."

"Who's she?"

"Byron's only legitimate daughter."

"Byron who?"

"*Lord* Byron. What are you, illiterate? He was the greatest romantic poet of all time."

"So what's his daughter got to do with the Department of Defense?" Academicians could be so tedious.

"She had a long romance with Charles Babbage, the man who designed and constructed the first calculating engine, way back in the 1860s, I think. Calculated logarithms, mostly, to the nth decimal. And Ada actually wrote the first sequences of numbers on which it based its calculations—so she was the first computer programmer, really. Then Babbage invented a typesetting machine and printer that would print out the computer's

132

calculations directly, without the intermediary of a human typesetter. That's what they were after, ultimately—a way to eliminate human error."

"A computing machine that bypasses human error."

"That's why the Defense Department named their program after her—that's their ideal."

"That's a long way from 'Ozymandias.'"

"Byron didn't write 'Ozymandias,'" Reingold stressed with some forebearance. "But I suppose I know what you mean."

Outside, the skyrockets were abating, party horns flagging, auld acquaintances wheezing their last chorus.

Jordan tapped the screen. "So this is a Defense Department study."

"Arguably," conceded Reingold.

Jordan kept tapping the screen, vaguely in time to "Auld Lang Syne." "'We'll take a cup of kindness yet,'" he hummed, tapping. Tapping the edge of the screen, the top of the console, the card slot at the side of the terminal. "Hey, what's this?" Jordan noticed the card slot for the first time.

"What's what?"

"This slot—this is just like the slots on the hospital terminals that take passcards."

Reingold inspected closely. "It does look like . . ."

Jordan took Breen's ID badge off his lapel, turned it over. On the back was an iridescent rectangle. He waved it in front of Reingold. "Laser identification—eliminates human error." He slipped the badge into the computer slot. Perfect fit.

He cleared the screen, and punched up number 1. Funding.

The screen went blank for five seconds, ten seconds . . . then suddenly lit up with the first of many long pages of legalese, beginning "Whereas the United States Government contracts with Genenco, Incorporated, to develop an echovirus variant strain . . ."

"Bingo," whispered Jordan.

"Incredible," said Reingold, in a dreadful hush.

They read two pages in silence, documenting that a numbered government bureau was to pay Genenco a certain amount per annum to research certain echovirus mutations, with the goal of developing a multivalent vaccine with which to inoculate soldiers being sent overseas, to prevent the poor performance displayed by enlistees who suffered from bouts with this transient but annoying common upper respiratory virus. There was much more information about the franchise of the project, under the heading of Funding, but Breen's card apparently wasn't cleared for access to it.

Jordan skipped the Genetics profile, and went right to 3Ai. Complications, Medical, Pathophysiology.

They read the first summary paragraph:

Echovirus Strain 121 was originally engineered to enhance certain variants' known potential for bleeding diatheses, first in conjunctival, and latterly in nasal membranous tissue, since it was these complications which led most often to disability in humans inoculated with the viral particle, in both experimental and clinical settings. Strain 121, however, has demonstrated the induction of a capillary fragility not limited to mucus membranes, but including diapedesis in, and rupture of, capillaries in the inner ear, optic chiasm, and brainstem—particularly in the areas surrounding the decussation of the cerebral peduncles. This has led to the unanticipated side effect, in some experimental subjects, of cerebral hemorrhage.

Jordan reread the last sentence three times. "They designed a virus that causes bleeding in the eyes, ears, nose, and brain," he muttered, stunned, unwilling to grasp it in full.

Reingold wouldn't grasp it at all. "It's impossible to believe they actually infected experimental subjects with such a thing. Human subjects, I mean."

"Impossible to believe!" Jordan grabbed Reingold's arm with all his pent-up anger and fear. "Look at my eye! Breen's already *died* of it, and Chessie . . ."

"Slow down, you were *not* an experimental subject, so let's not jump the gun on this," Reingold calmed him, but his gaze was not calm.

"Fecum devolvitur," Jordan muttered. Shit rolls downhill. The third law of medicine, after *Fecum non carborundum.* And once it starts rolling, it goes faster and faster, picking up more shit along the way, until it lands, finally, on the guy at the bottom of the hill. And Jordan suddenly had a momentary flash: The distant rumbles outside weren't celebratory fireworks; they were the trembling of the hill.

Unnerved, Jordan punched up 3Aii. Epidemiology. I. Case Retrieval. What appeared was the same list Jordan already possessed—the access codes to hospital computers across the county, a monitor of the diagnosis of every patient who entered.

Jordan went to 3AiiII. Cartographics.

What showed up now was a map of Los Angeles, with three colored splotches superimposed eccentrically over it, each color coded at the top of the screen:

YELLOW AREAS—NASAL HEMORRHAGES
GREEN AREAS—CONJUNCTIVAL HEMORRHAGES
RED AREAS—CEREBRAL HEMORRHAGES

It was the graphics of the spread of the epidemic.

Jordan slumped, his will collapsed. "This thing has leaked into the general population."

CHAPTER 9

"It can't be . . ." Reingold had turned pale.

"A virus that causes bleeding in the brain is loose in the city."

"My God." Reingold sat down hard on the desk. "My God."

"I'm going to die," whispered Jordan. He held the moment, cupped it in his palm like a fleeting treasure, a melting snowflake: this small, cubical room, shades of white and gray; the black holes in the acoustical tile ceiling, like a negative of the open night sky, its galaxies and stars; the hum of the computer, the flat odor of the centrally conditioned air; the look of bewilderment on Reingold's face, the hard linoleum floor; the Formica desk on which Jordan's fingers rested, the weight of the earth beneath his feet, the immensity of his feeling; and then, like an afterthought, one last skyrocket explosion outside. As if the battle were over, lost. Unconditional surrender. "I'm going to die," he repeated.

"You think I'm not?" Reingold snapped. He seemed to pull himself together all at once, mentally slapped himself. "In case you forgot, *nobody* gets out of here alive."

"So what've I got—three days? And Chessie may last

through the night. . . ." Walls were closing in, options running out.

"Look, just because you may be infected doesn't mean you're going to die—look at these graphics—some cover *just* nosebleeds."

"At least you *admit* to an epidemic now."

Reingold nodded judiciously. "It does appear that someone, here at Genenco, got contaminated in the lab—human error, again—and probably just spread it to whomever he came in contact with . . ."

"Breen," Jordan shook his head, nearly speechless.

"And I suppose this serial killer thing was just a red herring," Reingold shook his head. "Doesn't seem very parsimonious, does it? Still, people crump every day for different reasons, and look much the same in the end. 'Doctor, doctor, will I die?' 'Yes, my child, and so will I.'" He seemed to find great tragedy in the matter, if from a somewhat Olympian perspective.

"Will you stop being so goddam poetic and tell me what you plan to do about all this?"

"Well, first of all, we have to suppress it."

"What?" Baffled outrage.

"For the time being, I mean," Reingold explained. "We release this information tomorrow, and we'll have uncontrolled panic. I assure you, more people would die in traffic deaths trying to evacuate the city than would ever succumb to the virus."

"What do you suggest, then?"

"We've got to organize help for the victims, first— we'll designate three hospitals as our control points, we can do the triage from . . ."

"Don't call the Feds, whatever you do."

"No, no, it's county jurisdiction—I'll have to call peo-

ple off the listeriosis business, no way around that . . .
maybe get Ventura County involved . . ."

"Okay," Jordan agreed tentatively, "we won't go public yet . . . but let's get a printout of all this." He tapped
the computer screen. "Just for the record," he said,
thinking: just for the epitaph.

Reingold looked around. "No printer in here. Anyway, that could take hours, and we've got to get . . ."

Suddenly the security guard was standing in the doorway, testing an apologetic smile. "Sorry—could I get
you gentlemen to sign in? Totally slipped my mind."

"Human error," Jordan accorded graciously. "Happens
all the time."

"No problem," Reingold was already walking out the
door. "We were just leaving, anyway."

Jordan turned off the machine, slipped out the floppy
disk, pocketed it. As he stood to leave, he noticed a
building directory lying askew at the edge of the desk.
He picked it up on his way out the door.

At the security desk in the main foyer, Jordan stooped
over, signed Dennis Breen, time in and time out. Then
he wished the guard a Happy New Year, and joined
Reingold outside.

"So how do you want to do this?" said Art.

"You go home and work out a battle plan. I've got to
find Chessie."

"I could use your help in . . ."

"Not now!" Jordan cut him off. Silence filled the vac-
uum, then Jordan spoke more softly. "Look, I've got to
be alone a while, there's too many impulses colliding up
here." He tapped his forehead.

Reingold nodded once. "Call me in the morning."

And they walked off into different parts of the night.

138

The four stages of dying, Jordan had learned in medical school, were denial, anger, bargaining, and acceptance. Now, during this one long day, he'd zipped through a crash course in the first three, and still felt totally unprepared for the final.

Denial had nurtured him through the reddening of his eye, attributing it to his winter blepharitis, to the Santa Anas, to fatigue. And denial had been his first gut response to the revelations in the computer: No, this can't be. Even though he knew it was.

And then anger. At Breen, the fool, the supercilious purveyor of death. At Genenco, for being so sloppy. At the Defense Department, for funding such a stupid project. At himself, for contracting the disease. At Chessie, for giving it to him.

Chessie. Her eyes and nose had shown the telltale bleeding first; and Jordan had gotten close to her, had become intimate . . . and now this. The Big This.

Yet he'd felt better with Chessie, more whole, more alive—in her arms, having coffee across a table, telling a joke, watching her face, catching the mingled odors of soap on her skin—better with Chessie than he'd felt in years.

He had to have that with her again before he died. Before she died.

So that was the third stage—the bargain he struck: He would find her, he had to find her, tonight, before it was too late. And *if* he found her, *then* he would accept his imminently mortal condition.

Maybe.

In a small, dark room, on a small, dark bed, Chessie shivered uncontrollably. Bed-shaking chills, true rigors.

Her bones felt damp, as if they would never dry, as if their moisture were a permanent state, like the dew on a dungeon wall, permeating her flesh, condensing on her skin in a thin night sweat.

She'd never felt so bad. A febrility of spirit made everything at once hyperacute and distorted, as if her parts were fitted on wrong. Her teeth chattered, her nose ran, her skin was raw, it seemed that it must be inside out. There was a dull throbbing behind her eyes, made worse if she looked left or right. Her ears were ringing. She had to move slowly or she became quite dizzy, consequently she didn't move at all, simply huddled in the corner, on the edge of nausea.

Chessie was afraid.

She wanted to be unconscious, but was afraid she wouldn't wake up; wanted to go home, but was afraid Billy would find her; wanted to cry, but was afraid she couldn't stop, and afraid she wouldn't be able to listen for footsteps outside.

She heard a footstep outside. Billy? She crouched lower on her strange bed, tried to hold her breath, to hear better, but her respirations were too rapid and shallow, she couldn't control them. She saw a shadow pass the window; she peeked around the curtain. Nobody there, just the shape of a tree branch bobbing in the night. Just nerves. Just fear. No Billy come to drag her home, only the echo of his threat, and her bubbling fever: the virus, incubated, slavering in her deepest recesses.

She wiped her nose with her hand: mucus and blood streaked her cold finger.

From a darksome corner of her mind came this inkling, this image: herself, bleating, inverted on a great hook, eyes protruding, straining to understand the Faceless One who approached her, hand upraised, in a hollow wind.

It was after one by the time Jordan pulled up in front of Dolores's, tense and focused. Gilroy, sitting in his own car across the street, jumped out to meet him on the parkway.

"Sorry I'm late," said Jordan.

"Time flies like an arrow, but fruit flies like a banana," Gilroy joked, too excited to complain. "I'm really onto somethin' now, I found a coke dealer who . . ."

Jordan held up his hand. "This thing's opening wide up—they've let a genetically engineered virus escape."

Gilroy's eyes went wide. "*Who* has?"

"Place called Genenco." He began walking up to Dolores's doorstep, Gilroy right at his side.

"Slow down, man, what're you talkin' about, what kind of virus?"

"Kind that makes you bleed, and Chessie's got it, and I've got to find her, and I mean tonight."

"But this makes no sense, man, the coke story is panning out right down the line."

"I'm not saying there's not a connection—maybe the cocaine got contaminated with the virus, I don't know."

Gilroy's eyes acquired a rhapsodic glaze. "Buddy, this story is begging to be spilled. . . ."

"Not yet," Jordan said curtly, annoyed at Gilroy's barely repressed joy over the calamity. "The lid is on until Reingold can orchestrate some kind of disaster plan."

"Okay, but you gotta fill me in on these details."

"Essentially what I've said." They reached the front porch. The light was still out. Jordan knocked on the door. "How about the drug angle?"

"Dealer I saw had eyes like a bloodshot zombie, said everyone snortin' this stuff looks the same. Said it's a red hot pistol of a shipment, came up through Matamoros. And *then* guess what?"

Jordan rang the bell, knocked again. Still no answer. "What?"

"Guy had a seizure, right in front of me. Hit the deck twitchin'."

"What'd you do, call the paramedics?"

"Yeah, eventually. Searched his place first, though. Stole his address book, been callin' the numbers, made a couple promising contacts . . ."

"You let him convulse while you ransacked his apartment?" Jordan banged on the door hard enough to vent some frustration.

"What am I, a doctor? Listen, we're trying to save maybe a thousand lives here."

"Just two, tonight, all I want is two tonight," he whispered.

"Holy shit," Gilroy mused, "what a way to stop cocaine use in the country, just kill all the users."

"Kill all the users . . ."

"Yeah, what an ultimate law-and-order tactic—I mean, it avoids all the expense and time of like random urine tests, job firings, rehab programs, all that shit. Just gets right to the root of the problem: Do drugs, and die. There's a simplicity to it."

"You're not suggesting the government is intentionally lacing shipments of cocaine with deadly . . ."

"*Elements* in the government, maybe."

"That's preposterous . . ." he whispered, without much enthusiasm.

"Ever hear of paraquat? Ever hear some politicians say we should keep spraying it on the marijuana crops even

142

though it causes lung disease, because it serves those dope-smokers right if they . . ."

Several apartments down, the manager opened his door, roused by all the commotion. He eyed Jordan and Gilroy suspiciously a long moment, then walked across the courtyard toward them, carrying a large flashlight.

He was a small, older, near-sighted, belligerent man, wearing a bad wig, and a hearing aid connected by a long wire to its battery pack clipped on his dirty undershirt. When he reached them he shone his light in their faces and spoke with a slight, vaguely European accent.

"I'm the concierge. What the hell do you two want?" His tone was surly, his sweat territorial.

Jordan was long practiced at falling into role, though—the ER had trained him to be alternately kind, intimidating, cajoling, authoritarian, or concessionary, as the occasion demanded. So he instantly transformed his anxiety into officiality now—and without missing a beat, took out his wallet and flipped it open to show his ID. "I'm Dr. Marks, this is Dr. Gilroy . . ."

The manager focused his flashlight down at Jordan's array of certification cards: his medical license, D.E.A. license, hospital photo-ID.

Jordan continued speaking. "My patient, Dolores Reed—a tenant here—is in critical condition. We urgently need to examine her apartment for empty pill bottles, environmental toxins, that kind of thing. . . ."

The manager inspected the impressive documents a moment longer, then took the ring of fifty keys off his belt, his voice now reluctantly apologetic. "Well. That's another pair of sleeves, then. It's just that, you know, there's been lots of funny goings-on in this unit . . ." He unlocked the door, giving Jordan a meaningful nod, like a fellow professional.

143

Jordan looked understanding. "Like what?"

"Burning the midnight candle at both ends, if you ask me." Then, confidentially: "I think they got an unauthorized tenant living here, too." He pushed the door open wide, and led the way in.

The three of them stood in the darkened entranceway as the manager fumbled for the light switch. It clicked, finally, but no light came on. Click. Click. Click. They stumbled in a group through the shadows to the living room.

The air was thick with that peculiar absence of something, breath or ions or thoughts—but the sense was unmistakable: No one was here. The manager turned on a table lamp, light filled the room. No dead bodies. Everything seemed okay.

Jordan thought it best to keep the manager on the defensive. "You use asbestos insulation here? Some of these old places, people inhale the asbestos . . ."

"Hey, mister—doctor—I'm not the owner, I just run the place."

Jordan spoke as if by the book. "Would you mind checking the bedroom first, make sure it's not occupied?"

"Gladly," said the little man, and stole quietly up the hall, half hoping to get a glimpse of something raw, Jordan suspected.

When the manager was gone, Gilroy spoke in a whisper. "Guy's got the worst toupée I ever seen."

Jordan began searching every surface for paper items, which he would glance at, then toss. "We're looking for an address book, an envelope . . . anything that might have Dolores's contact to wherever Chessie is being hidden."

Gilroy turned up the cushions, dumped a couple

144

drawers, grinned like a scamp at Jordan. "Pure and simple journalistic know-how."

"Can't wait to see your writing style, you show such style in your investigations."

"Style never won the ballgame, buddy. Hey, she have a Rolodex? Or a kitchen bulletin board?"

The living room was picked over; time to move on. "Phone's in the kitchen," said Jordan. "You check there, I'll check the bedroom."

They both moved down the hall. Gilroy went on to the end, to the kitchen, while Jordan turned into the first side room off the corridor. The den.

The light was on. It was small, obviously recently converted into makeshift sleeping quarters, obviously recently where Chessie had been staying. There was a single mattress on the floor, an open suitcase in one corner. A bureau and chairs were pushed up against the opposite wall, dirty laundry piled on one of the chairs.

The manager, rifling through the open closet with a look of glee and vindication on his face, clearly had his own agenda on this foray. He stepped out, holding up one of Chessie's dresses—two sizes too big for Dolores. "I *told* you there was an unauthorized tenant living here—the woman who signed the lease is a size three . . ."

Jordan ignored him and proceeded to open and close bureau drawers, go through Chessie's mostly empty suitcase, upend the wastebasket on the mattress.

The manager continued, undaunted by Jordan's aloofness. "This is a seven, at least." He waved the dress like a matador's cape. "I was a tailor thirty-two years, they think I don't know these things?"

In an ashtray, Jordan saw the red matchbook he'd watched Dolores take from her skirt at Sarno's, when she was waitressing. He picked it up now, stared at it. It read "Dinah's."

Gilroy, meanwhile, was exploring the kitchen. He found a couple of possible numbers on a chalkboard near the wall phone and scribbled them down on his notepad. He opened and closed some drawers. He saw some mail on the table, went over to examine it; stood, sorting through it, with his back to the side of the refrigerator, his back to the space between the refrigerator and the wall . . . where the crumpled, twisted body of Dolores was wedged, her neck broken, her eyes open in some ghastly, silent horror.

When he finished going over the uninformative lot of mail, he turned, moved to the front of the refrigerator, opened the door, and peered in. He stuck his hand inside, rustled around, shifted some food; and the body settled a fraction, just the other side of the appliance.

Gilroy grabbed a beer, closed the door, popped the top. "Time flies, fruit flies . . . and barflies like a good brew." He smiled, sucking back a mouthful.

The body behind the icebox silently awaited flies of its own.

Jordan finished his search of the den and moved on with the manager close on his heels.

"What about the bathroom?" the man suggested. "You looking for pills, you check the bathroom. I don't want to tell you your business . . ."

Jordan forced himself to smile and nod. He wanted to maintain his facade with the guy, even though the manager's interests varied from prurient to manipulative.

So he crossed over to the bathroom, opened the medicine cabinet. The manager, almost licking his lips, was trying to see over Jordan's shoulder; but Jordan was blocking the view as well as he could.

"What is it, pills?" said the manager.

It was the usual assortment of home remedies, cold prescription bottles, Valium, Gantrisin, Darvon, Lotrimin suppositories, a comb, a diaphragm, some Bactine, a box of Band-Aids . . . and a cluster of cocaine paraphernalia. Mirror, spoon, straw, razor blade, and a small, brown glass vial full of powder.

Jordan confiscated the vial and closed the cabinet without letting the manager see. "Where's the bedroom?" he said, forcing the man to turn around and exit the bathroom ahead of him, giving Jordan the moment he needed to pocket the vial.

They entered the bedroom together. The light was already on, from the manager's initial intrusion. There was a single window, a bay window, and beside it a low, queen-sized waterbed; a matching fifties dresser, chair, and desk, blond wood, well used, probably her high school set; and a walk-in closet.

The manager walked in, apparently to inventory. "Thirty days' notice, that's what these people get . . ."

Jordan went through all the drawers and surfaces, increasingly frustrated, hope fading to a scream. If he couldn't locate Dolores or her contact in the underground women's network, he didn't think he had a prayer of finding Chessie. Dolores had let one private joke slip, though. "She said someone she sees every night at bedtime," he muttered.

"What?" the manager attacked, coming out of the closet. "*Who's* in her bed every night?"

Jordan tried to re-create it, kept his mind fluid, walked to the bed. He was vaguely aware that the manager was staring at him. "Hmm? Who what? Oh, the pills. The empty pill bottle must be at the bedside."

His time was short, now, he knew: The manager had gotten what *he* wanted, and was now viewing Jordan with renewed suspicion. Jordan willed the man out of his consciousness, though. He just lay down on the waterbed, on his back, and looked all around: the walls, the ceiling, Gilroy who was just entering, swigging a beer—all rocking slightly, from Jordan's perspective. Then he rolled over on his side, to look out the window. And there it was.

The only thing visible from this angle was the high pink neon sign on the bar two blocks down: Dinah's.

Jordan sighed a sigh the size of the meaning of life.

"You feeling yourself?" said the manager.

Jordan rolled himself out of bed. "Think I found what we were looking for."

The manager looked down at the base of the bed, near the window where Jordan had been staring so intensely, and he suddenly became very nervous about his sick tenant. "Hey, look, if you're worried about the roach-killer we sprayed around the baseboards, that was the owner's decision."

Jordan smiled officiously. "We'll notify you."

Jordan exited. Gilroy began to follow, waiting for explanation until they got outside; but the manager caught him by the arm and smiled deferentially. "Doctor—please—" he tapped his breastbone—"My wishbone hurts. All the time. Can you give me some advice?"

Gilroy beamed ingenuously. "Just stay away from the angel with the flaming sword, buddy." Then he winked, and left.

He met Jordan at the car a few moments later, as the

manager walked back to his own unit. "What'd you get?" Gilroy asked.

"It's a long shot," said Jordan. "Here, take this, though." He handed Gilroy the tiny vial of cocaine. "Get it to your friend in DEA, or vice, or wherever, for analysis."

Gilroy held the container up to the streetlight as Jordan removed the Genenco directory from his pocket and began riffling through it. Gilroy tried to evaluate the nature of the powder in the orange glare of the sodium arc. "You really think this blow could be like contaminated with a virus?"

"I wouldn't taste it to find out." He tore one of the pages out of the directory, gave it to Gilroy. "This has Harris's name and address on it—he's the executive director of Genenco."

"King of the Germs." Gilroy perused the page.

"Yeah. Find out what you can about the guy—his training, his background, associations with drug agencies, intelligence agencies . . ."

"Maybe ease on down and do an exclusive commando interview tonight, get it on 'Sixty Minutes.'"

"I told you, no press yet." His nose was getting all stuffy; he took out a handkerchief.

"Mike Wallace, watch out," Gilroy couldn't help needling.

Jordan knew he was being needled, he was simply in no mood to banter. Too much was happening, too much was too real to be playing games. "Yeah, fine, just be careful, I told you the CIA may be involved." He blew his nose.

Gilroy heard CIA and clenched his right fist with a big good-ol'-boy grin, trying to contain how tickled he was. "I love it," he whispered.

Jordan finished wiping his nose, and looked down at the hanky: it was spotted lightly with blood. "Shit," he said, low and mean. He began walking away, to the end of the block. "Meet me in a few hours. In the ER."

"Where you goin'?" Gilroy called.

"I need a drink."

CHAPTER 10

Even from the sidewalk, Jordan could hear a major party going on inside. White Christmas flocking opacified the windows, tiny colored lights blinked on and off all around the door. Cardboard signs were tacked up across the front:

Merry XXmas
Happy No Y

He hoped Chessie's contact's name was actually Dinah, otherwise he wasn't sure how he was going to approach the problem of locating someone whose face and name he didn't know, in the middle of a New Year's party at a loud bar. The stakes were high, though, so nothing to do but forge ahead.

He forged ahead, into the bar.

Inside, it was three times as loud, twice as dark, the air thick with cigarette smoke, sweat, perfume, alcohol. Jordan was immediately aware of an electricity to the atmosphere, a sexual tension that energized him, brought him alive, alert; but he wasn't certain why until he walked slowly farther in, toward the dance floor, and his eyes accommodated to the dark: Everyone here was a woman.

This was a gay bar.

There were a dozen couples dancing, a couple dozen more sitting at tables, twice that many standing around, a score at the bar. All women.

Some looked tough, some yups, some chic, some New Wave, some in costume, some cool, some hot. And no men.

Except Jordan. Jordan ordinarily had few opinions of any kind about peoples' sexual proclivities or life-style preferences. Anything was okay with him, as long as it was mutually agreeable among the parties involved. And this was quite a party.

He tried neither to gawk nor cower. He tried to maintain his cool as he sauntered up to the bar. And above all, he tried to keep, in the forefront of his mind, his long-held belief that if you just acted like you belonged somewhere, people would tend to accept it. But oh, it was hard.

He was getting lots of stares, and he knew it—the eye pressure was almost palpable. Some were hostile, some amused, some curious, some appraising. He understood, for the first time, how a woman feels walking past a construction gang.

He reached the bar feigning as much nonchalance as he could muster, as if he was just stopping in for a drink, or something. He leaned on the bar top, put one foot up on the brass rail. Flanking him on the barstool to the left was a woman who looked like a fashion model out of *Vogue,* and on the right, a surly punk-queen in leathers, who might have been the bouncer. Just beyond her were a couple of sweet-looking girls, one in Osh-

Kosh overalls, the other in jeans and a workshirt. That's good, thought Jordan. It's a mixed kind of place.

The bartender came up to him—a cute, young, smiling lady wearing tight Levi's, a white tank-top undershirt, hoop earrings, and a mop of short hair. "What'll you have?"

He was so off balance, the question took him by surprise. "Uh . . . bourbon on the rocks . . . uh, on ice." He hoped he hadn't offended anybody yet.

"Comin' up." She went off to fix the drink.

Jordan looked around. No sign of Chessie or Dolores. He felt as if everyone in the place were either whispering, or pointedly ignoring him, though he also suspected most of the people here could probably have cared less. His gaze finally came around to the punk-queen sitting next to him. She stared back icily.

"Nice place," he said.

She eased off her seat as the bartender returned with Jordan's drink. "Buck-fifty."

Jordan took out a pad of paper, flipped it open, pretended to check names on it—it was, in fact, as blank as his game plan—and then formally smiled at the bartender. "We're looking for a . . . Chessie Lewis or a Dolores Reed."

"We who?" said the bartender, losing just a shade of geniality.

"Board of Health," said Jordan. "Dolores said maybe Dinah could help me."

"Dinah who?" Her brightness was back.

Jordan tried to look patient, though his greatest fear was beginning to rise in his gullet—that the first sign of resistance would crumble him. "Listen," he said, keeping the quaver out of his voice, "we think Chessie might be very sick."

"Maybe she ought to see a doctor."

"I *am* a doctor." He was sorry already he hadn't kept his story strictly factual.

"Lemme guess," the bartender smiled. "Gynecologist."

She strolled to the other end of the bar as Jordan nodded, understanding he'd have to start over. He sipped his bourbon, glanced to the right—the punk-queen was gone now, replaced by a jolly, overweight lady in a Santa Claus costume, drinking an Irish coffee. Jordan nodded pleasantly at her.

"Santa Claus was a woman, you know," she explained as if she were making a point of information, her purpose to enlighten.

"No," Jordan cleared his throat, "no, I didn't know that."

"Sure. Santa Barbara, Santa Clara, Santa Rosa—the Santas are all women. The men are all San—Diego, Francisco, Luis Opispo, Raphael, Anselmo, they're all San. Santa Marta, Santa Lucia, Santa Claus—those were the women saints. Cheers," she toasted and drank.

Jordan downed his bourbon. "You don't know Dolores Reed, do you?"

Santa shook her head. "You really a doctor?"

Jordan raised his eyebrows up and down, pulled his stethoscope out of his jacket pocket where he'd stuffed it on his way out of the hospital earlier today—it seemed like a year ago—and dangled it back and forth before Santa's eyes. "You're getting sleepy," he intoned, "you're going to tell me where to find Chessie Lewis."

Santa laughed—just as in the poem—like a bowl full

of jelly. Jordan had to laugh, just to hear her. He put his stethoscope away.

"You must've appreciated our sign out front, then," said Santa, wiping her eye. "Two X's in Xmas, as in two X chromosomes."

"And no Y," he smiled, getting it for the first time.

"Just a joke, son," she patted him on the back. "Let me buy you a drink, to prove no hard feelings. Me, I don't dislike men. Just like the company of women better."

"Me too," he agreed.

She called the bartender. Then, to Jordan: "What do you want with this Chessie Lewis?"

He considered. "Want to try to save her."

"From herself, I suppose?" An echo of sarcasm, now—unbecoming on Santa Claus.

"From human error," Jordan smiled sadly.

"Ah, but to err *is* human."

"Yeah, I want to tell her that, too."

A finger tapped him on the shoulder. He turned to see the punk-queen motioning him to follow her, with no joy in her expression. Jordan put two dollars under his empty bourbon glass, and shook Santa's hand. "Maybe we can play doctor sometime."

The twinkle returned to her eye. "Next New Year's Eve, same barstool, come early," she beamed.

Jordan joined the punk through a door at the end of the bar, into a corridor that curved around behind the bar. It was a long, semidark hallway, at the end of which was a pay telephone. They passed a door marked Bathroom—the door just closing on several women inside—and stopped at the next door, which was closed

155

and unmarked. Jordan's escort knocked twice, opened the door, and ushered him through.

He found himself in a small, elegant office, facing a tall, sophisticated, forty-five-year-old woman. She wore a black evening dress and pearls; but there was a toughness about her, too, in the lines around her mouth and eyes, a sense they came from much laughter and much pain.

The room itself suggested a similar internal tension: a couple of exquisite Victorian pieces, an oriental rug, Diane Arbus photos on the wall; a pedestal, down-lit by a low-voltage high-intensity museum light, exhibiting a shattered crystal champagne glass.

At the far end of the room, another door was half open. Beyond it, a small, private party was in progress. Leaning in this doorway, somewhat behind the woman who stood at her desk facing Jordan, was a second woman—this one a twenty-five-year-old, pretty, no-nonsense urban cowgirl, wearing designer jeans, cowboy boots, and flannel shirt, and watching Jordan's entrance without expression.

The punk-queen, having shown Jordan in, now left again, closing the door behind her. Jordan smiled tensely at the club owner, who made no overtures.

"You must be Dinah. I'm Jordan Marks. I'm here to find Chessie Lewis."

"You her husband?"

"Her husband is dead."

This seemed to surprise her, which sent a jolt of excitement through Jordan: This woman knew Chessie, knew her problem. He was close.

"You a cop?" said Dinah.

He shook his head, but hesitated. How should he play it? His instinct was to come clean, but something about

156

the woman intimidated him. He needed some weight. "Board of Health," he said. Which wasn't really untrue, he was working with Reingold, now.

"See your ID?" she challenged.

He showed her his medical license, as he'd shown the apartment manager. Dinah was more self-assured than the manager, though, and certainly brighter. "This says you're a doctor," she spoke as if she were clarifying the point for him. "Doesn't say you're Board of Health."

"I'm here on my own time."

"On your own time, I don't like you pestering my employees and patrons."

"I just need some help," he pleaded, starting to sweat.

She studied him a moment. "What makes you think *I* know where she is?"

"Dolores told me."

She pitied the lie. "Dolores would *never* tell a man her contact.

Again, so close. He stepped forward, urgency in his voice. "So you *do* know where Chessie is."

As soon as he advanced on Dinah, the cowgirl in the doorway took two quick, protective steps in reaction. They both reached the desk at the same time, Jordan in front, cowgirl to the side. In the silence of the face-off, Jordan was suddenly aware of sounds just beyond the wall that separated them from the bathroom—flushing, giggling, talking.

Behind her desk, Dinah seemed totally at ease, in control. "You a friend of her husband?"

"I'm a friend of *Chessie*," he insisted. "I'm afraid she may be terribly ill, and not know it."

Dinah smiled indulgently at the cowgirl. "Now *there's* a con I haven't heard . . ."

"This is not a con!" shouted Jordan.

Dinah remained cool, if not cold, though. "A man will say anything to get even with the woman who finally sees through his bullshit."

The cowgirl, made loquacious by such wisdom, spoke for the first time. "You got *that* straight."

Jordan could see he needed a new approach. He took his pen out of his pocket, leaned down to the desk, and wrote on the back of an envelope lying there. "Look, here's my name, my work number at the hospital, and my home number. If you *do* hear from her, and she *is* sick . . ."

He stopped speaking so he could concentrate on the telephone that sat on the desk beside his hand. The number stamped on the dial was upside down from his frame of reference, but he read it anyway, and memorized it: MO5-6772. When he was certain he could keep it in his mind, he stood up and handed Dinah the envelope on which he'd written his own phone number.

She took it, deadpan. "Next time I'm feeling self-destructive, I'll give you a call," she said.

He nodded, thinning his lips, and departed. As soon as he closed the door, he walked quickly down to the end of the hall, to the pay phone on the wall. He stuck a quarter in the slot, covered the mouthpiece with his hanky, and dialed the number he'd just memorized in Dinah's office.

The phone rang once, and was picked up. Jordan whispered clandestinely through his handkerchief, in a medium-register raspy voice. "Some man was here about Chessie Lewis," he said, "and you gave him my name!"

In the earpiece, Jordan heard Dinah answer, heard the outrage in her voice. "I did no such . . ."

"Call me in a minute," Jordan whispered. "Can't talk

now. Call me person-to-person, through the operator, and use my *full* name, so I'll know it's really you."

"But I'm not even sure I *know* your full . . ." Dinah began, but Jordan hung up.

He pocketed his hanky, walked quickly back up the hallway, past Dinah's office, to the bathroom next door. Then he took a deep breath, checked his fly, opened the bathroom door, and entered.

A number of women were either surprised, amused, or annoyed by his entrance: Two were sharing a joint, one was putting on lipstick, two were making out, one was exiting a toilet stall; another stall looked full. Jordan immediately put one hand to his stomach and the other to his mouth, looking as if he were only moments away from throwing up. Then he lurched across the bathroom to the nearest stall, which shared a wall with Dinah's office.

He entered the stall, locked the door behind him, leaned over the toilet, took his stethoscope out of his jacket pocket, put its earpieces in his ears, its bell against the wall. With his free hand, he pulled a pen and scrap of paper from his pants and brought them to the wall beside the bell of the stethoscope. Pen poised, he listened intently.

And thirty seconds later, extremely muffled, from the office next door, he heard Dinah's voice: "Yes, I . . . no, that's right . . . will . . . calling five-zero-six, five-seven-four-seven, person-to . . . Ms. Barbara . . ."

Jordan wrote the number down as he heard it, but the last name was obliterated by a barrage of scuffling sounds at his back. He turned to see the door of the stall being jimmied open with a penknife. Feet proliferated under the door.

He yanked off his stethoscope, stuffed it back in his pocket with the pen and paper, and sat down on the toilet, trying to look sick. A moment later the door was flung open by Dinah's cowgirl, who immediately pulled him upright by his lapels, jerked him out of the stall, and slammed him against the wall.

It knocked the wind out of him; cracked the back of his head against the tile, too, made him see lights, made his legs a little rubbery. Faces crowded all around him, scowling, murmuring, tilting. The strain of what he was about, the bourbon, the viral syndrome, the head knock . . . he felt stunned. Almost out-of-body.

Her face filled his visual field. He pushed her back, hard, against the stall door. Enraged, she backhanded him across the face. He brought his hands up, after the fact, leaving everything below his nose unprotected. Cowgirl half crouched, came up with a potent undercut, and punched him in the balls.

He doubled over, incapacitated. Slumped to the floor. Various impressions crossed his sensorium: mingled voices, a couple gasps, a few claps; pain that drowned out all thought, pain inside pain, like a shearing of nerves that had been asleep all his life until this moment, a whiff of urine as his cheek settled onto the cold, tile floor; a sense of motion, of scraping and bumping, as he was dragged out of the bathroom.

Then feet all around his head—were they going to trample him?—as he was dragged down the carpeted hallway. His eyes were open, now, he realized: the carpet was dark red, thick with cigarette ash and street grime. He'd have coughed, but his diaphragm was still paralyzed.

He felt the procession halt abruptly. A door opened. A cool breeze hit his face. The ice locker? Were they going to freeze him to death? Without warning, he was air-borne, and the next moment skidding unceremoniously across the gravel and bottle shards of the back alley. As he came to a stop against the dumpster, he looked up to see cowgirl and punk-queen standing over him. They each kicked him once—one in the ribs, one in the back—but it seemed more out of a sense of completion than necessity. He'd surrendered way back on the bathroom floor.

They walked back to join their minions, and slammed the door shut on the man who lay crumpled in the garbage, unmoving, hoping it was over.

He remained still for two or three minutes, letting the night wake him slowly. His shirt was torn, his lip bled. Gradually, breath returned; he moaned quietly, testing his voice, and scared away a cat that was nosing around. His hands, holding his crotch, were afraid to let go. The pain had subsided just enough to let nausea emerge now, so he threw up. This made the pain worse again, forcing him to be still for a few more minutes.

Finally, by great effort of will, he moved his left hand from between his legs to his jacket pocket. He made a fist around everything in there, brought his fist up to his face, opened the hand: The pen and the stethoscope fell to the ground; what was left in his hand was the scrap of paper, still containing the phone number he'd scribbled down in the bathroom.

He clenched his hand around the paper, and began the slow process of sitting up.

Walking was so painful he had to pause and regroup after each step; but he told himself pain meant he was alive, which was more than he could say with certainty about Chessie. So he kept moving.

161

It began to rain, too, which helped revive him. Just a spattering, really, little more than heavy mist. He tilted his head back, opened his mouth, caught a few cool drops on his tongue, and on his face. Felt like being a kid again, like catching snowflakes. That was the problem with L.A., there were no snowflakes in the winter. Snow he could do without—snow meant shivering, and scraping ice off the windshield, and snow chains, and dead batteries; but snowflakes were a different matter, a great loss in the paradise of southern California.

Jordan closed his eyes, and pretended he was catching snowflakes on his tongue, first snow of the year, the air cold and clean and new. That was it: For just a moment, Jordan felt new again.

Then he opened his eyes, and it all came rushing back. The pain, the garbage, the end of life.

He hobbled to the end of the alley, to the street. Cars whizzed by, full of party animals. Someone stuck her head out the back window of a passing Trans-Am and vomited. Jordan thought: I guess it's just that time of night.

He walked two blocks, slowly, until he reached a carwash with a phone booth at the corner of the lot. The giant sign posted high above the drive-in entrance read Free Psychotherapy with Hot Wax. Jordan wondered giddily if they did autohypnosis. A patrol car crawled by, down Vermont, prowling. Jordan straightened himself up, tried to look less disheveled, eased into the phone booth, shut the door, rested against it, panting from the exertion. That's all he needed, was to get busted now.

He picked up the receiver, pulled the crumpled paper from his pocket: 506-5747, Barbara. That wasn't the number he dialed, though. He dialed 911. The city emergency aid number.

The phone rang twice in the receiver, then Jordan heard the voice come over the line. "Nine-one-one. State your emergency, please, and the number you're calling from."

Jordan hesitated. His intention had been to trace the phone number in his hand to an address. The central computerized switchboard had cross-referencing capabilities such as that, and Jordan had made use of them in the past, when he was working in the ER, to locate the phone number of some concussed, amnesic patient, or the address of some disoriented overdoser.

But he'd forgotten that as soon as you called 911 and the line connected, the phone number and location you were calling *from* flashed up on their computer screen. This was done for two reasons: first as a life-saving measure—if someone called them but couldn't speak (inhaled a marble, burglar in the next room, whatever), they would immediately dispatch emergency vehicles to the address that lit up; and second, if the caller told them he was calling from a different number from the one he was actually calling from, they'd know it was a prank, or a crank, and treat it more skeptically.

Jordan's problem now was that he had no authority, in this phone booth, to find out from the emergency switchboard the address of a woman named Barbara, with a certain phone number. He could tell the switchboard he was a doctor, but talk was cheap. He could say he was calling from the emergency room, and they'd probably just send that prowl car back to the phone booth to interview him. His breathing was becoming heavier, too, the more locked-in he felt, and he knew that wasn't helping his credibility any.

The switchboard operator spoke again, calm, helpful. "Is this a police, fire, or medical emergency, please . . ."

Jordan hung up, wiped his nose on his sleeve. Blood and snot. Time was burning.

He walked the three blocks back to his car, limbering up along the way. The pain in his balls was receding a bit, and localizing, allowing the pains in his ribs and back to blossom. He wondered if there'd be any blood in his piss, though just the thought of urinating made him gag and nearly retch.

It was almost two-thirty by the time he pulled up to the entrance of the ER. Definitely much the worse for wear, he got some funny looks from everyone as he limped in, bruised, bloodied, and torn; but he ignored them, left them to what he assumed would be massive speculation, and walked straight into the doctors' office, closing the door behind him.

He slumped in the chair, picked up the phone, push-buttoned 911. It connected in the middle of the second ring.

At the 911 central switchboard, one of the operators picked up his phone. The computer screen in front of him lit up with the following information: a small street-grid of the city, with a blinking light at one pair of cross streets; the address of Bay Cities Hospital, which was the location of origin of this call; the phone number of Bay Cities ER, which was the phone number of origin of this call; the time on the twenty-four-hour clock, which was 0229; and the date, 1/1/86.

The operator registered this all as he spoke into his phone. "Nine-one-one. State your emergency, please, and the number you're calling from."

"This is Dr. Marks, at Bay Cities ER," said Jordan, falling easily into role, in this chair, in this room. "The number here is three-four-three, eight-two-one-two . . ."

The operator verified this as the number that had

been alight since circuit contact. "Yes, doctor, what's the problem?"

Jordan stared at his paper fragment, the paper-thin hold he had on Chessie. "Problem is," he spoke in his most relaxed, professional tone, "we just got a call from a patient of ours—one of our repeaters—stating she'd just overdosed, at the home of her friend, 'Barbara.'" He put concern in his voice, but also a touch of buddy-buddy for the 911 operator, who was probably a moonlighting paramedic—as if to say, "We know about these drug users and their friends, don't we, operator?"

"What kind of overdose?" asked the switchboard man.

"Who knows?" said Jordan. "Now, all we have *here* on this Barbara is a phone number, which is five-zero-six, five-seven-four-seven . . ."

The operator hit a key that cleared his screen, then punched up the phone number Jordan was reading to him. Three seconds later a name and address appeared beneath the phone number:

BARBARA ENGEL
634 CITRUS AVENUE
L.A.

Beneath that, a street-grid with a blinking locus.

Jordan was still speaking, ". . . so we need the cross-listing, to dispatch someone Code three . . ." Code three was lights and sirens, life-threatening emergency. Assuming Chessie was there.

"That listing is for Barbara Engel, at six-thirty-four Citrus Avenue in L.A., sir . . ."

Jordan wrote the name and address down in trembling hand on the same shred of paper he'd used to transcribe the phone number.

"Would you like me to dispatch a paramedic unit to the scene, doctor?" the operator inquired.

Jordan closed his eyes, controlled his words tightly. "Yes. Please," he said softly. "Thank you."

Then he hung up and wept—sobbed, for half a minute—took a few deep breaths, wiped his face on a surgical gown, tucked in his shirt, and walked back out to the car.

CHAPTER 11

Gilroy started up the long walk of Dr. William Harris's huge Brentwood residence. Its immaculately landscaped lawn was full of shadows, cast by the low-voltage pink and yellow Malibu lamps uplighting the bougainvillea, star jasmine, juniper. Granite statuary and privet topiary were scattered across the grounds, like mythic beasts lying in wait.

Gilroy reached the front door and rang the bell. Thirty seconds passed. Deep in the upstairs of the house, he heard a stirring. He lifted the heavy brass knocker, let it fall against the door, twice. He waited. A light went on. Footsteps approached.

Gilroy saw the peephole above the knocker turn from light to dark as someone behind the door peered through it at him. "Dr. Harris?" he said brightly. "Thomas Gilroy here. I'd like to speak with you a moment, if I may, sir."

"What do you want here?" came the muffled, guarded voice.

"Dr. Harris, I'm here tonight following a lead for Channel Eight Update News, and the first question I'd like to ask you, sir, is: Is it true you doctors always bury your mistakes?" He gave the peephole a big smile.

Behind the door, Dr. Harris stood in a dressing gown and slippers, looking stern and rudely awakened, though still, for the hour, quite civil, his hand hesitating on the doorknob.

Stern, rudely awakened, quite civil, and in this dark light, seemingly quite bald.

Jordan sped down Wilshire Boulevard, heading east, past Beverly Hills. Traffic was fairly light at 2:40 A.M.; but the intermittent drizzle made the streets slick. With so little weather most of the year, a layer of oil, grease, and gasoline slowly accumulated over the pavement, like a sheen, laid down by the millions of passing cars; so when the first water of a light rain mixed in with it, a slippery suspension was created, a La Brea Tar Pit for cars.

Jordan had already run a couple of red lights, once swerving to avoid another car he'd cut off at the crossing. The swerve turned into a ninety-degree tailspin, but he brought it around, back in control, and eased his foot down on the accelerator again. It just opened his eyes a little more, that's all; woke him up.

He wore his stethoscope around his neck, now, so if a cop tried to stop him for speeding, he could simply wave the stethoscope, avoid the detainment. Doctor on emergency. Might even get a police escort out of it.

Which was okay with him, at this point. He was banking on Chessie being at this address, at Barbara Engel's place. She'd only been missing for a day and a half, she wouldn't have had time to get very far into this hidden network, wouldn't have had reason to go farther, really. Billy Lewis couldn't have penetrated this deep,

and that's who she was hiding from. Jordan did not believe in a just and benevolent God; but he prayed, nonetheless, that he was right. If he was wrong, he didn't
think he had the resources to pursue the matter further.

His hope was that he'd arrive at the house right after
the paramedics roused everyone out of bed. The paramedics would either leave, with Chessie—which was
fine, Jordan could trace her easily to the nearest hospital—or they'd leave without her, which meant she'd be
up and talking with Barbara, trying to decide what to do,
when Jordan arrived. Jordan, the lone cavalry soldier,
saving the wagon train. Just like General Custer.

He turned up Citrus, past Crescent Heights, ten minutes later. It was a dark, quiet, residential street, single-
family dwellings in the old Spanish style, with red tile
roofs, pink or white stucco walls, lots of archways,
mini-haciendas. Halfway up the block, a paramedic ambulance sat in the driveway of 634, its cherry light flashing silently. A few people could be seen standing on the
front steps, under the porch light, talking. Jordan pulled
up to the curb in front of the house, shut off his engine,
sat, and watched.

The ambulance was parked right behind a new Volvo,
which was pulled up tight to the closed garage door. The
garage was contiguous to the house, which was a nice
but not lavish one-story affair, in the mode of the other
homes on the street. The front porch was less than ten
steps from the driveway.

Standing there talking—arguing, it looked like—to
the paramedics was a woman Jordan took to be Barbara
Engel. She appeared to be in her early forties, well-
heeled, wearing a conservative but elegant party dress,
something from Saks or Nordstrom's. She held a small
boy asleep on her shoulder, dressed in pajamas with ei-

ther cowboys or 'droids on them, Jordan couldn't tell which from this distance.

Engel looked angry as she rocked slowly from foot to foot, trying to keep the boy asleep. The paramedics looked confused, maybe apologetic. Almost as soon as Jordan cut his ignition, Engel turned around, entered the house, and closed the door behind her. The paramedics shrugged, started back down the steps toward the ambulance. Jordan got out of his car and met them at the rig.

"Hi guys, I'm Dr. Marks." He smiled. The stethoscope slung limply around his neck—bell over one shoulder, earpieces over the other—was his best credential.

"You the doc that phoned this in?" said the driver.

"Yeah, what's the story?" said Jordan.

"No story, no patient—this lady was just getting home when we arrived, and she denies anyone sick being in this house."

"Someone must've been jerkin' your chain, doc," said the other paramedic.

Jordan felt his stomach turn over, like he was losing the ball at the one yard line. "Did you ask to look around? Might be someone in there against their will."

"Not my detail, doc—I can patch you through to LAPD in the rig, if you want . . ." He nodded at the ambulance.

Jordan eyed the house, inventing tactics. "No, I guess not."

"Yeah, forget it," the driver agreed. "Lady's a lawyer, and she already sounded pissed off."

"Okay, thanks, fellas," Jordan nodded with a you're-off-the-hook smile, "have a good one."

"You, too, doc. Hasta lumbago," said the driver.

"Affirmatory, same old story," said the other paramedic, and laughed.

They got in the rig, turned off the flashing cherry light, backed out of the driveway, and rumbled off as Jordan walked back to his car and stood in its shadow, staring up at the house. Beside the front door was a large, arched picture window, covered by white curtains that were dimly lit, as if the living room were dark, but a back room light was on. In front of the window was a narrow garden of tall shrubs and manicured bushes.

Jordan silently walked up the lawn, to the bushes, then along the front of the bushes to the side of the house. He peered around the corner, down the side: back at the rear of the house, a light, probably from a bedroom window. He walked back along the streetside bushes, up the two porch steps to the front door. He put his ear to the door. Silence. Probably putting the kid down, getting herself ready for bed. Looking in on Chessie? Waking Chessie to tell her something very strange just happened, maybe they ought to make a call, get Chessie situated somewhere else? Letting Chessie sleep?

He walked over to the Volvo, sitting snug against the garage door. He put his hand on the hood, then drew it away—the hood was quite warm, it had been more than a short drive. He looked up at the house again. He had to get inside.

Sneaking inside seemed like the best plan now. Find Chessie if she was here; and if she wasn't, find the next clue to her whereabouts. He looked at the tall hedge that fronted the house, stopping at the porch. He looked at the car again. What he needed was a diversion.

He walked to the back of the Volvo and crouched down beside the rear bumper. Then he took his beeper off his belt. It had served him well as a diversionary device in the past; he hoped it would work now.

He flicked the button to memory mode, and slid off the black plastic side, revealing two AAA batteries. Then he slowly bent back the front panel until it snapped off, exposing the inner workings of the beeper—wires, chips, tone generator, the underside of the batteries. Robot guts.

He pushed the button at the top: The machine began emitting a regular, continuous series of beeps. Then he reached under the car, and with the belt clip-on that was still attached to the back of the beeper, he hooked it onto the inner edge of the bumper, hidden from sight. Finally, he stood and ran back to the front door. Putting his ear to the door, he vigorously rattled the knob, waited, and jiggled it again. Back at the car, the beeping was faint but distinct. He turned the doorknob one more time, then hopped down into the bushes beside the porch, and huddled into the leafy shadows.

Seconds passed. Twenty? Fifty? The beep goes on, he thought. There seemed to be some stirring at the front curtains, beside the door; or maybe not. Jordan's heart double-timed the beeper. He wasn't sure he could tolerate this level of tension much longer; no, he was sure he couldn't.

The front door opened. Half obscured by shrubbery, Barbara Engel stepped out onto the front porch, looking grim. She wore a long, black velvet evening dress, matching shoes, with an emerald brooch and bracelet, a hint of Chanel No. 5. Very dressy, very tasteful. Jordan liked the look, and in a spasm of brief, temporary insanity, he very nearly complimented her. Get a hold of yourself, man, he thought.

She heard the beeping—Jordan suddenly thought it

must be audible as far as San Pedro—and looked at the car. If it sounded enough like a bomb, Jordan assumed Engel would evacuate the house.

Cautiously, Engel stepped down from the porch and inched out into the front yard, over the lawn in a wide arc around toward the rear of the car. Gutsy lady, thought Jordan. When she was several yards away, with her back to the house, he silently crept in the open front door and scurried into the house without being seen.

He had to do this quickly, he knew. Fast as he quietly could, he tiptoed from room to darkened room, looking only for the shapes of people. Living room—piano, couch, chairs, all empty, tables clean and Deco. Dining room—table, chairs, rocking horse, cabinet. Kitchen— dirty dishes on the table, nobody in the chairs. He turned past the refrigerator . . . and ran into a human shape, gasped, jumped, knocked it over; it bounced up again, one of those inflatable Bozo clowns. He nearly had a heart attack on the floor, paused several seconds to regain his equilibrium, and went on.

Long, dark hallway, past a little Deco phone stand, past the bathroom—nobody in the bathtub or on the toilet—past a book-filled den, its chairs empty, nobody sleeping on a mattress on the floor. Then more hall, to the first bedroom.

It was dark, but Jordan could see at once a long thin figure asleep on the bed against the far wall, under the covers. Chessie's shape. He snuck to the bedside, crouched on the bed, put his hand on the sleeper's shoulder. "Chessie . . . ," he whispered.

She turned, but it wasn't Chessie, it was the young boy, still 90 percent asleep. "Mommy?" he muttered out of his dream.

Jordan stroked the boy's head, unnerved but still tender. "Shhhh . . . back to sleep," he whispered, rolling him back over to the well-nestled pillow.

From the front of the house, Jordan heard a muffled voice. He tiptoed to the bedroom door, strained his ear, but couldn't quite hear the words; so he peeked around the doorframe. There at the head of the corridor, Barbara was speaking on the hall phone situated on the low Deco table he'd passed. She had her back to Jordan, facing the open front door; in her other hand she held a small dark object that might have been the beeper, quite silent now.

Jordan looked across the hall. Directly opposite the room he was standing in was the door to the master bedroom, softly lit. This was the light he'd seen from the outside of the house.

He held his breath, and scuttled across the hall into the room. It was a beautifully designed place, half-Deco, half-Nouveau, bedlamps that were black marble women holding glowing globes, a black teak queen-sized Deco bedframe, peach wallpaper, jade green carpet, Erté prints on the wall.

Jordan sat on the bed. A few legal journals lay open at the bedside, along with a Z-channel cable guide, a TV remote control panel, a Chinese amethyst figurine, a decanter of Madeira. Jordan silently picked up the phone on the bedstand, covered the mouthpiece with his hand, and listened. The first voice he heard was Engel's.

". . . anyway, I think it may be a homing device, in which case he may now know where you are."

"Well, Dave should be back with the boat any minute, and then I'm outta here . . ." came the voice from the other end, more distant, raspy, covered with static from the approaching electrical storm—but almost certainly Chessie.

Almost. Jordan started to say her name, then held back, jumpy, second-guessing himself.

Engel said into the phone, "Just keep your eyes open, there's something very fishy . . ."

Jordan stood, unable to sit still . . . and knocked over the amethyst figurine. It fell to the floor. It wasn't very weighty, but it was delicate, so it broke with a soft tinkle. Soft, but loud enough to stop all conversation.

"Shit," Jordan mouthed. He tossed the phone on the bed, ran five paces to the window and threw it open as Engel's footsteps grew louder running down the hall toward the bedroom. He climbed onto the window sill, and was half in, half out, when Engel appeared at the bedroom door.

"Freeze!" she shouted.

He looked directly at her. She stood facing him, in pistol-range firing stance, holding a .38 revolver on him, steady as a statue in black velvet. So that was the object she'd been cradling in her hand—not the beeper, but a gun. For the second time today, time seemed to stop for Jordan: this room, its elegant appointments; Death, the Seductress, pointing a black, hollow finger at him.

Jordan jumped. Barbara fired. The window shattered as he hit the ground outside, rolled twice in the damp grass, and pushed up running.

He sprinted along the side of the house, toward the front yard. Behind him, Engel leaned out her window and fired off three more rounds. Jordan tripped over a tricycle, thought he was hit—fell, scrambled to the corner of the building, made the turn.

Neighbors' houselights began to flick on.

Jordan raced across the front lawn flat out, made it to his car, jumped in, and started the engine as Engel reached her front door. He put the car in gear, screeching tires, fishtailing several times before he straightened out, picking up speed. Engel shot again, and again, the second bullet smashing through Jordan's rear window and exiting the front left side window, right by his head, shattering the glass completely out of the frame. He careened around the corner at last, out of sight and range.

Speeding west on Wilshire, back from where he'd come, back toward the beach. He was giddy with fear, relief, dread, elation. Laughing, his teeth chattering, his hair blowing wildly in the wind that rushed through the blasted-open windows. Sweating, hyperventilating, gripping the steering wheel against the rain-slicked highways. He was a mess.

And he still had to find Chessie. So close. He'd heard her voice—disembodied, reaching to him. Ahab's, that's where she had to be. Waiting for Dave to ferry her somewhere to safety. Except Dave didn't know she needed a hospital . . . if even that would save her. Dave just didn't know she needed Jordan.

He was coming apart, he could feel it; but he couldn't let it happen, not yet. Not until he found her. So close.

He got to the docks in record time, lurched to a stop, ran down to the pier where *Ahab's Ride* was moored. But the slip was empty. Jordan clenched his fists, would have torn his hair, literally, if his hands had been near his head. "No . . ." he moaned, so inarticulate it sounded animal, primal.

He looked up the boardwalk to Ahab's Basement. The place seemed dark. He stumbled over to it, gazed in the windows, his nose to the glass. All dark. He tried the doorknob . . . and the door sailed open at his push, ringing the ship's bell once as it did so. Uncertainly, he stepped inside.

The room was thick with the obscure, sinister shadows and shapes of carved figureheads, broken anchors, prognathic jawbones, rusted machinery. It amplified the sense he had that this was all a dream, had all been a dream, all day. Dream, or more specifically, *pavor nocturnis*—night terror. A demented kind of special nightmare, composed of feelings without image, horrors that leave no residue of memory save the sickly boding that they will return.

But this day was full of images. Maybe it was a near-death experience, then, or maybe he already *was* dead, and today was the first level on his descent into hell.

His foot creaked on a floorboard, snapping him back to reality. "Chessie?" he whispered. "You here?"

He took two more steps toward the back; around a huge old cracked rudder; past a weirdly painted wooden dolphin. "Chessie . . ." he rasped more loudly.

He was about to call out when a net was thrown over him, and he felt himself pushed hard into a pile of buoys and tackle. He went down with a crash, completely off balance.

He thrashed, trying to twist free of the netting, but a heavy workboot shoved him in the chest. He fell back again, more junk tumbling onto his head.

And then before he could even kick at it, he saw the whaling harpoon swing around on him, advance on him, its point come to rest on the small of his throat.

The third time, death. And this time Jordan's reserve was gone. His muscles went flaccid, his eyes closed; there was almost a measure of peace. He was so tired. Three times; death always came in threes. In the ER, it was always three cardiac arrests, three DOAs. If there were only two, you always waited for the third. And Jordan had felt death's breath twice today—with the computer, reading the echo program; then the velvet and emerald woman with the gun; and now, the spear tip at his throat, pressing deeper, he felt it denting the skin, in a moment it would take him, like the serial killings, actually, with a sharp object plunged up the base of the neck, except those were from behind, and this was from the front, but either way, his life would soon be void, and merciful blessing, he could rest at last. So he'd reached the fourth stage of dying, it seemed, after denial, anger, and bargaining: acceptance.

And then a voice came out of the darkness, from the figure who wielded the weapon; a voice staccato and gravelly with fear, anger, and phlegm: "Billy Lewis, I am nobody's victim . . ."

And either Jordan was hallucinating completely, or it was Chessie's voice.

CHAPTER 12

"Chessie . . ." Jordan barely dared to breathe. "It's not Billy. It's Jordan. I'm Jordan."

There was a rustling, and the light went on. And there was Chessie, one hand on the switch, one on the harpoon, poised in fear and uncertainty, the whites of her eyes red as the berry of the hollywood.

"Jordan, my God, I thought . . ." She tossed the harpoon to the side, kneeled to disentangle him from the net and help him up.

He hugged her. "Thank God you're okay. I was so scared you'd be . . ."

"I'm okay. I'm okay."

He kept hugging her, didn't want to let her go. Her warmth calmed him, restored him. He would survive, now; they both would, with care. He had to get her to the hospital fast, though: There were only a few hours left to the end of her sixth day of symptoms.

She was shaking. Her fever had lysed, the crisis of delirium was past, temporarily; but she looked pallid, drawn, ten pounds thinner.

She touched him over and over with trembling fingers, to make sure he was real. "I thought you were Billy. I thought you were going to hit me again." She was too wired to cry. "I couldn't stand the thought of that. I would have killed you first."

Jordan paused, smoothed her hair. "Chessie—Billy is dead."

She stared at him intensely, trying to assimilate this news. Joke? Accident? A jangle of emotions flooded her face: disbelief, doubt; justice, relief, guilt; grief, fear.

She tried to speak, but her throat was thick. She could only shake her head, and ponder the night.

They got to the emergency room at 3:45. On the way over he told her what he knew and what he suspected, coloring her confusion about Billy's death with a new shade of anxiety. Her visions of Death had not been totally delusional, then. The Faceless One still scratched at the door.

The ER was quiet when they arrived. Jill Fergus was the doctor on call, talking sleepily to the night nurse. Jordan and Chessie, at point-blank range, made quite a pair: strung out, on edge, his clothes torn, her clothes matted with sweat, eyes glazed with recent delirium and sheened with blood.

Jill grinned brightly at them. "Wow—did you two just come from Russ Hall's party?"

"Jill, you know Chessie." Jordan needed to get right to the point.

"Sure, hi."

"Hi," said Chessie.

Jordan let his worry show. "Do a complete work-up on her, will you? Neurological, SMA-24, culture up her nose and eyes, anything else that strikes you."

"Sure," said Jill, tightening her brow. "What do you suspect?"

Jordan winced. "Echovirus." He was superstitious

enough to worry that saying it made it real. The power of language.

Jill escorted Chessie to one of the acute beds—the gurneys in clear view of the nursing station—and drew the curtains around them for privacy. She began conversing with Chessie in low tones, as Jordan just stood where he was, a dozen feet away, zoning out in the wake of his longest day.

Good God, what was he going to do now? They were together, that was the main thing; but what if she died now? Sudden stroke, how could he stop it? Stroke, because it was like a stroke from God, one moment healthy, alive, the next moment . . . struck. Struck down. Struck out.

It made all his whining about being forty seem so feeble to him now. Big deal, BFD, forty years old, only forty years to go. Not like forty hours, or forty minutes. It drew the perspective of his natural life out to the horizon, to the vanishing point.

Vaguely, he was aware of the voices behind the curtain.

"So what are you feeling, exactly?" Jill was saying.

"Like . . . my ears popping," said Chessie. "I dive a lot, and right now it feels like I'm having a pressurization problem, you know?"

Jordan's eyes slowly came into focus; he squinted at what he'd heard.

"Something with your equilibrium?" Jill asked Chessie.

"No, not exactly. Pressure equalization is the closest I can come to describing it. Something with my pressure . . ."

And suddenly something clicked for Jordan. Something about her choice of words, the way it gelled with

181

words in some of the charts he'd read earlier in the day. The power of language again.

He ran back into the doctors' office. The epistaxis charts were still piled high on his desk. He sifted through them quickly, looking for the first one he'd gone over—Cheremoya. Here, Cheremoya. He opened it to the ER sheet, scanned it to look for the vital signs. *Pulse, 124. Respirations, 36. Blood pressure, 80/40 initially, falling as low as 60/0.*

Low, dangerously low BP. Jordan flipped through the nursing notes of Cheremoya's entire hospitalization. Nowhere had his pressure gone above 110/70—still relatively low.

He turned to the very front of the chart again, to the Discharge Summary. To the last sentence: *Discharged home, doing well.* Doing well.

He went to another chart. Dennis Breen. Just a few pages thick. He turned right to the first ER sheet, and his eyes fell immediately on the blood pressure: *160/100.* And under the heading Past Medical History, the word *hypertension.* High blood pressure.

And Jordan knew well enough what Breen's discharge summary was. Discharged to the ECU. Eternal Care Unit.

He opened Billy Lewis's chart, to the ER sheet from a week ago. *BP 150/95.* And further down: . . . *mild hypertension, probably related to cocaine abuse* . . .

Jordan felt his pulse thumping in his neck. The solution was quickening.

He opened another chart. Normal blood pressure, normal discharge, alive and well.

Another chart. Minimally elevated blood pressure, patient developed rapid onset of left-sided paralysis, cerebrovascular accident. Transferred to a nursing home.

Another chart . . . but he didn't even read it, he jumped up and ran from the room, to the curtained-off bed where Jill was beginning to examine Chessie.

"It's her pressure!" Jordan exploded. "What's her pressure?"

Jill looked at the chart. "It's a tad up," she shrugged, "one-thirty over ninety. All this excitement, though, I'm not surprised."

Jordan wasn't listening any more, though, he was getting IV utensils from the shelf—catheter, tourniquet, bag of dextrose in water. "I want her on a nitroprusside drip," he ordered, "her systolic pressure not to exceed one hundred. I want a private-duty nurse, and a monitored room . . ."

Jill looked confused. "Jordan, what's the deal?" A BP of 130/90 wasn't all that high; certainly not serious enough to warrant the use of nitroprusside, a potent agent for lowering malignantly high blood pressure.

"Yeah, Jordan," Chessie echoed with a weak smile, "what's the deal?"

He wrapped the tourniquet around Chessie's arm, palpated for a vein. "The deal is, the virus by itself is relatively harmless. It's the virus *plus* high blood pressure that's fatal."

Chessie's voice sounded dry, far away. "How high is fatal?"

"I don't know," said Jordan. "That's why I'm keeping yours way down."

Jill went to tell the nurse to mix up a bottle of nitroprusside as Jordan punctured a bulging vein in the back of Chessie's left hand with an eighteen-gauge intracath, then withdrew the needle stylus and plugged in the IV tubing.

183

"Oh," said Chessie, trying to think low-pressure thoughts.

It was a private room, 412, down the hall from the CCU. Chessie lay on the bed in a hospital gown, the IV dripping into her arm through an Ivac, a small computerized box connected to the tubing, to regulate the rate of administration. On her chest she had patches fastened to wires that led up to a cardiac monitor above the bed, beeping her EKG pattern on a small, green oscilloscope screen. A blood pressure cuff was wrapped around her right arm, connected by rubber hoses to a digital readout that continuously monitored her pressure, systolic showing in one window, diastolic in the other. Systolic was the top number, the pressure head generated by the force of the heart's pumping, the pressure Jordan wanted to keep below 100. It now read 98.

"I feel like somebody's science fair project," she said. She was trying to keep her spirits up, but Jordan could hear a fragile edge to her voice.

"Yeah, mine. I just drop a penny in the toilet, and you'll be copper-plated in ten minutes." He was methodically going over all the apparatus, checking the equipment to make sure everything was working properly—in the moment, and in case of emergency.

He checked the defibrillator against the wall, ascertained that the paddles were in their slots, pushed the On and Charging buttons, up to 400 watt-seconds, verified that the paddles could hold the charge, then pushed the button to discharge the current.

"What are you doing?" she wanted to know.

"Just checking."

"Why does this make me feel more nervous than safe?"

He walked, next, to the crash cart—the red steel multidrawer cabinet on wheels that contained all the equipment necessary to deal with any emergency that might arise on any patient: IV medications essential in cardiac arrest, intracardiac needles and syringes, endotracheal tubes, temporary pacemakers, tracheostomy sets, IV bags, laryngoscopes, CVP wires, chest tubes, bite blocks, peritoneal lavage trays, Kelly clamps, scalpels, manometers. Jordan went through the cart drawer by drawer, making sure everything was where it was supposed to be.

When he came upon some vials of medicine marked Inderol, he put together a needle and syringe, filled a syringe with the solution, and pointed the needle toward his face.

"Jordan, what are you. . . ?"

He squirted the medication into his mouth, swallowed it with a grimace. "Just making sure *my* pressure doesn't rise," he said. Inderol was a beta blocker, which kept both pulse rate and pressure reasonably low, at the appropriate doses. "And it tastes awful, so it must be good medicine."

He got in bed beside her, and they snuggled under the covers.

"I like your bedside manner," she said weakly.

"I like your bedside," he smiled. He held her close, pulled her face to his shoulder, smelled her hair. Smelled like being alive.

She stroked the back of his head, burrowed into his chest, would have crawled inside him if she could have. "Been a long day," she whispered.

And still not over, thought Jordan. Chessie was safe, now, and so was he; and he found himself thinking he had unfinished business at Genenco. They had docu-

185

mentary evidence of this epidemic over there, and they were withholding it from the public. And people were dying. Maybe not Chessie or Jordan, now; but people were dying, and those bastards were sitting on it.

Jordan found himself getting angry, quite angry. All his mounting tension, his frantic desperation, was quickly being funneled in one direction. Toward Genenco.

And a fear crept in, too. What if Reingold confronted them tomorrow, or the next day, and they denied it? In fact, certainly they *would* deny it. And they'd have all the time in the world to clear their computers, bury the evidence. Erase the disks, if necessary.

Of course, Jordan had one disk himself. But couldn't they claim it was a fraud? Couldn't some hacker have programmed it, as a hoax?

He had to go back. And he had to go back tonight.

The thought of it made him shudder.

"You're shivering," she said.

"I've got to go back to Genenco," he whispered.

"What—now?"

He nodded, but for a moment couldn't speak, he felt such loss at the prospect of leaving her side.

"Why?" she said.

"Sutton's law." It was another law of medicine taught on the wards.

"Which is?"

"Willie Sutton was a big-time bank robber, I think in the forties. He kept getting caught, though, and sent to prison, and then he'd escape and rob some more banks, and they'd put him away again, and he'd break out again, and rob more banks. And when they asked him why he kept doing it, why he kept robbing banks, he said 'Because that's where the money is.' That's Sutton's law."

She half understood. "You're still trying to get away with something."

He shook his head. "*They're* trying to get away with something."

She sighed. "Well, you can go to your bank tonight, but you better come back right here to your savings and loan in a big hurry."

He kissed her eyelid. "You okay?"

"Who knows? The man I hated most in my life is suddenly dead, *I* almost died, *you* almost died, my damn *eyes* are bleeding, you're leaving me alone to these predatory blinking machines, and you want to know if I'm okay. Are you for real?"

"Real enough." He felt a little tremulous once more. "I just don't want to lose you again . . ." He tried to embrace her, but the wires tangled them, the monitors went wild.

The door burst open, and in walked a thirty-five-year-old man with trimmed hair and beard. Charlie, the private-duty nurse. He stopped abruptly in his tracks when he saw what was going on in bed—startled, first, then amused. "Okay, you two—one foot on the floor . . ."

Jordan sat up, a bit sheepish. He'd requested that Charlie be the nurse here—they were old pals from the ICU and several famous hospital Christmas parties.

Jordan glanced over at the digital readout on the blood pressure monitor, and nodded to the nurse. "Evening, Charles. Just making a field test of some of the equipment here—and I'm happy to say everything appears to be in fine working order."

"If you're referring to me," Chessie said, "you haven't taken me out on the highway yet."

"And if you're trying to make me your straight man," Jordan countered, "you already did." He modestly readjusted his pants. "And as for you," he said to Charlie, "as your first official duty, you'd better increase the rate of nitroprusside infusion. I'm afraid I just raised her blood pressure."

"Don't flatter yourself," Chessie deadpanned.

Charlie smiled, read the BP monitor—systolic pressure 109—and turned up the IV as Jordan walked to the door.

Jordan locked eyes with Chessie. "Try to get some sleep. I'll see you soon."

"We never close," she smiled, "except our eyes." And she did.

He walked down the hall to the nursing station, got an order sheet off the shelf, and wrote out Chessie's admission orders—medications, diet, activity, and so on. The head nurse took it, thanked him, and began to transfer the relevant items to her Cardex as Jordan picked up the phone and dialed Reingold's home.

"Hello?" The voice sounded tired, half beaten.

"Art—we're going back. Tonight, before the sun. Now."

"Are you crazy?" Haggard incredulity.

"No, but I was stupid. I just realized I signed Breen's name when we left there, at the guard's desk. Anyone seeing that name in the morning will know there's been a security breach."

"So what?"

"So they'll destroy all the evidence."

"But we have the floppy disk."

"Disks can be forged. We have to go get the smoking gun, not the gun-owner's manual."

"What are you talking about?"

"The virus. We've got to go get a vial of that virus. The actual stuff. That's their smoking gun."

Reingold sounded scared. "But we *can't* go back there now—that guard will know something's up . . ."

"I'm going. I'd like you to come help, you know lab setups better than I do, you could probably find the plates faster. But in any event, I'm going. So if you have the time, be there in fifteen minutes."

"Don't do this . . ." Reingold pleaded, but Jordan hung up.

God*dam*, he was mad.

He walked the three blocks with his jacket pulled up over his head to keep off the increasing drizzle. Four-fifty; the streets were mostly deserted now. Parties done, hangovers still hours away, this was the middle earth, the time out of time. Resolutions hadn't yet given birth to regrets, and another year was newly dead. The year is dead, long live the year.

Long live us all. Jordan felt the cold drops sprinkle his face in the directionless wind. He felt totally alert, and potent. He'd just survived his own death.

And now he was going to burn these fuckers.

He waited in the shadows of the front door of the Genenco building, checking his watch every few minutes. When fifteen had gone by, he waited another three. And then no more. He clipped Breen's ID badge once again to his lapel, took out Breen's keys, and began to unlock the door. And then Reingold ran up.

They stared at each other—edgy, uncertain, keyed up—then both nodded, and entered.

Jordan shrugged like an aristocrat as they strode past the guard. "You get an idea, you gotta run with it, doesn't matter what the clock says."

Reingold smiled as if his face might crack, but the security man seemed satisfied, and went back to his novel. Jordan led Reingold once again through the double doors, into the main corridor.

He took the building directory from his pocket and leafed through it as they walked. They paused under a recessed ceiling light, so Jordan could read more carefully. Full of down-shadows, Reingold's face took on the aspect of a death mask.

Jordan pocketed the directory again. "End of the hall," he said.

They trotted down, Jordan in the lead, checking room numbers until he found the one he liked—156. He tried the handle. Locked. He tried Breen's keys. The second one opened it. Slowly, side by side, the two doctors entered the lab.

One wall was a bank of windows to another room. There were control levers on this side of the windows, remote-controlled robot arms on the other side, for performing tasks in the strictest isolation.

Two walls contained banks of incubators. The fourth wall was all computer.

The floor space was occupied by the machinery of biotechnology: ultracentrifuges, an electron microscope, spectrophotometers, racks of test tubes, petri dishes, autoclaves, pipettes, wire loops, radiation counters, agar gels.

They took it all in slowly, until Jordan finally nodded

at the wall of incubators. "It's got to be somewhere in there."

He walked over and began randomly opening the small, square, stainless steel doors. Behind them were shelf after shelf of vials, test tubes, and dishes of organisms growing in culture. All the incubators exuded a warm, vaguely sweet, stagnant air. Some were in darkness, some in red light, some in violet light, some in eerie blue.

The shelves all had labels.

RHINOVIRUS-II
ANTHRAX
HTLV-V
C. BOTULINUM
E. COLI
CYTOMEGALOVIRUS
RABIES VIRUS
KURU
ENCEPHALITIS-B16
RSV-13
ENCEPHALITIS-R33
EBV-7
RETROVIRUS-AO

Jordan read each label, slammed every door shut. No Echo-121 yet, and there were literally hundreds of doors. After the twentieth try, he stood there, unmoving, momentarily daunted. Reingold stood at the other end of the room, motionless.

Jordan ran over to a computer terminal, took out Breen's floppy disk, plugged it in. He began punching keys, but kept ending up with DOES NOT COMPUTE.

Angrily, he looked over at Reingold, who twitched in every direction at once, like a straw man in a high wind, his gaze flickering from one entrance of the room to the other, terrified of discovery.

"Hey, you know ADA," Jordan said. "Give me a hand here."

Reingold walked over, sat at the console beside Jordan, hit a series of keys, chose from the menu, punched more keys. The screen went blank; then lit up: ECHO-121: ROW 3, COLUMN G, DRAWER 6.

Jordan jumped up and ran along the wall, checking the designations, which were etched in the face of each door. Seven from the eastern wall, three up, just at chest level on Jordan. Door 3G. He opened it. Inside were shelves of drawers, a light violet glow, a waft of a fetid odor, yeasty, decayed.

"Okay," Reingold called out, "can we please get out of here now? I'm about to have a coronary."

Jordan ignored him, intent on his mission. With contained excitement, he located Drawer 6, labeled ECHO-121, and pulled it open.

It was empty.

CHAPTER 13

He just stared at it for what seemed like a long time. Tried to make the viral cultures appear by the intensity of his gaze. The drawer remained empty.

The drawer below it was empty, as well. ECHO-122.

"It's gone," whispered Jordan.

"Multiplying across greater Los Angeles, no doubt," said Art.

"But they'd have kept *some* in stock," Jordan shook his head. "It's been moved. And there's an ECHO–one twenty-two bin here but *it's* empty, too."

"Maybe they woke up and tossed the whole batch."

"Check it out," Jordan pointed. "On the computer."

Reingold shrugged rather hopelessly, and began prodding the program about 121, 122, and other possible strains extant. "Achtung, Herr Direktor," he muttered.

The guard stuck his head through the door. "Gotta sign in, gents," he reminded them with the gentlest of reprimands.

"Right you are," Jordan smiled, approaching the man with a wink. Passing Art, he said, "Keep it up," then joined the guard and accompanied him down the hallway, back to the foyer.

The guard sat immediately down to his paperback as Jordan leaned over the sign-in book. Leaned over, pen poised . . . and stopped, arrested by what he saw.

The last signature in the book wasn't his own, pseudonymously Dennis Breen, from earlier tonight; the last signature was Dr. William Harris, signed in just thirty minutes ago. Signed in, and not signed out.

"Dr. Harris is here?" Jordan spoke as neutrally as possible.

The guard looked up from his book. "Yeah, I assumed you were meeting him. . . ."

"Right . . . right." Jordan smiled wearily, as if this type of wire crossed all the time at his dizzyingly elevated level of mentation. "Where'd he go?"

"His office, I thought."

"Right . . . that's what he said . . ." Jordan shook his head in apologetic self-deprecation. "Thanks." He strolled back through the double doors, reopening his directory, flipping through it tensely. Dr. Wm. Harris, Office of the Director, 273.

Jordan trotted up there, second floor, end of the hall. Tried the door. It opened.

There was Harris.

He was a trim man in his early forties, his prematurely thin hair cropped close as a Marine recruit's— a branch of the service with which he still maintained ties. His skin seemed unusually swarthy to Jordan— looked like a winter casualty of a Beverly Hills tanning clinic. His dress was casual but preppy—penny loafers, Eddie Bauer pants, L.L. Bean flannel shirt, white cashmere sweater—which meant overdressed for the predawn hour, as far as Jordan was concerned. So: a preppy, Beverly Hills Marine doctor.

194

"Who the hell are you?" Harris demanded in a voice that filled all these bills.

"I'm the guy that busted you," said Jordan. His voice had no volume, his heartbeat was so thin, so rapid. His eyes were riveted on the object in Harris's hands: a gunmetal gray cylinder, two feet long, with a four-inch diameter. A transport canister for biologicals.

Harris clutched it defensively, though his tone remained aggressive. "You're unauthorized here, mister . . ."

Jordan nodded. "And you've got a box full of echos there."

Harris's hand went to the desk phone as Jordan rushed him. They hit the wall, knocking over a coatrack. Harris was in better shape, but Jordan was crazed, breathless. Harris went to the mat backward, striking the arm of his chair directly between his shoulder blades, rendering him momentarily motionless on the floor. Jordan got up quickly, holding the canister. It was surprisingly heavy, or maybe not surprisingly. He tried to unscrew the top, but it was held fast by a vacuum-seal clasp that required a special tool to open. And Jordan had a special tool. He reached into his pocket, pulled out the multifunction pocket utensil Abel the detail man had given him—trach blade, splinter forceps . . . nothing covering air-sealed biological transport container locks, but Jordan wasn't choosy. He opened out one of the tools at random, and jammed it forcefully under the latch mechanism on the tube's lid. The thing pried apart in a matter of seconds, unprepared for such an assault. Jordan had the airtight top unscrewed, but still in place, by the time Harris lurched to his feet.

"What are you doing?" Harris rasped. Jordan lifted the

195

top. "Don't open that!" the director directed, suddenly pale under his suntan.

Jordan replaced the cap—just resting—with a grim emptiness in his eyes. "Like a faceful?" he asked.

"No, don't . . ." Harris raised his hands, trying to protect himself, across the room, from Jordan's incompleted threat.

"No?" Jordan professed surprise. "Nervous about a little inoculum of—" he peered theatrically at the small label affixed to the bottom of the steel tube—"strains one twenty-one and one twenty-two?"

"I'm not afraid for myself," Harris spoke slowly, reconstructing his deliberate composure. "It's the *project* you mustn't jeopardize." He took a pack of cigarettes from his shirt pocket, stuck one in his mouth, offered one to Jordan. "Mind if I smoke?" The civilized barbarian, gracious in defeat. Jordan shook his head, declining the invitation while allowing the vice. Harris shrugged, put away the pack, and lit up with a long, needlelike battery-operated electric cautery device he picked off the desk, its tip red hot at the push of a button. "So what is it you want, exactly?"

"I want to know."

"What?"

"Everything." He tipped the canister earthward.

Harris twitched. "I spill the beans, or you spill the gravy, is that it?"

"That's it."

Harris considered. "And what do you know already?"

Jordan briefly outlined what he'd managed to discover. "That's some of what I know," he concluded.

"You're a doctor, it seems," Harris said, drawing on his cigarette.

"And you call yourself one," Jordan tried to regain his

196

momentum. "But you've just let this thing progress, you knew people were dying . . ."

Harris looked strained. "You're way off base . . ."

Furious, Jordan cocked his arms back, ready to spew the contents of the container all over Harris and the walls.

Harris flinched, raised his hands to his face, and for a long moment the two of them froze in this tableau, like an old etching, the bookplate illustration of a moral cautionary tale. Then, tentatively, they relaxed a fraction; but the balance of power in the room had shifted now. Advantage, Jordan.

Harris finally shook his head, as if his ball had just taken a bad bounce. "The problem was, you see, the pilot study was done on young, healthy army volunteers—and *they* just came down with *nosebleeds.*"

A minor mistake, an annoying glitch, thought Jordan. "So it wasn't until the virus accidentally spread to the civilian population that you realized the blood pressure complication." Of course, young army recruits wouldn't have had any hypertension, so none of them would have bled into their brains. "Not exactly," Harris explained. He paused, as if making a decision, then continued more in the old-boy mode—doctor to doctor. "You see, the army was testing a new vector. . . ."

A vector was an infinitesimal migrational droplet that carried germs through the air, for germ warfare purposes. The vector was the vehicle to which a microorganism was attached, to get the germ where it was going, airborne. The vector was the microscopic missile; the virus was the warhead.

"Testing the vector with this echovirus?" Jordan asked.

Harris nodded. "Genenco was hired to design a virus with an easy marker to follow—like nosebleeds—so it could be sprayed in a small area. Then the epidemic would be easy to keep track of, by just searching for that diagnosis in hospital computers. Billing computers were easiest. Then once you see how fast the epidemic spreads, you can get an idea of how well the vector works."

Jordan, dawning, was aghast. "You're not saying you . . . intentionally sprayed this virus over our own civilian population?"

"Not sprayed, exactly, no. More like . . . released. From repositories that wouldn't arouse much suspicion, say something as innocent as . . . oh, a child's balloon."

"You made guinea pigs of unknowing American citizens?"

Harris became annoyed. "Grow up, doctor. The Russians are ten years ahead of us already, the way we've been hamstrung by you bleeding hearts. As far as I'm concerned, the people who died here in this exercise were soldiers, and they died for their country. These were patriot deaths, pure and simple."

Jordan tried to press it rationally, or ethically, tried to cool his bitterness. "But once you *did* know about the complications, you could have lowered people's blood pressure with drugs, until the danger period was over, until the virus ran its course."

Harris dismissed this out of hand. "Blood pressure had to rise over one-fifty before there was any real danger." Then he smiled, not quite apologetic. "Besides, bad press is bad press. This project had to keep a low profile, or . . ."

"This is *crazy*!" Jordan raised his voice unexpectedly. "You'll never get away with this! You have the hubris to think no one will believe me on this matter? I intend to . . ."

"I hope to convince you otherwise," Harris placated. "We're not just madmen, you know. The release of

E–one twenty-two—tomorrow—is designed specifically to field test a vaccine we've developed . . ."

"Tomorrow . . . ," Jordan echoed. His arms were beginning to ache under the weight of his burden.

"If successful, it could give us the capability of vaccinating everyone in the country *before* we released the more virulent strain . . . on an invading army, for example."

"That's so sick," Jordan shook his head. "The serial *killer* is not this psychotic."

Harris raised his hands in protest. "The serial killer was *not* my idea, I refuse to take sole responsibility for that decision." He grew more anxious again; sweat beaded on his upper lip.

Jordan did an internal double take. Like a solution finally precipitating, the idea formed in his brain; a physical thing, a visceral understanding. Was it possible? Was this maniac before him evil on so many levels—could he deal death by hand as well as policy?

"Of course, the *idea* of the serial murders was sound," Harris went on somewhat academically. "The needle in the brain muddied the waters, so to speak—it contained the epidemic by isolating and neutralizing the carriers in such a way as to obscure the original cause of bleeding in the experimental subjects."

"In the *people*, you mean," Jordan corrected him, stunned. "The human beings."

"It was a last resort, believe me. Quarantine would have been my first choice—quarantine the carriers, accelerate the disinformation campaign. We planted some very good leads suggesting this was a cocaine problem, for example; and then we set up the epistaxis hotline, *that* was my idea, as a way to keep track of anybody

199

who was getting suspicious." He looked pointedly at Jordan. "The snoops of the world . . ."

"Didn't work," Jordan said bitterly. "The snoops won. This is going to be front-page news tomorrow."

Harris just shook his head. "If you're talking about that 'nosy' newsman—Gilroy?—I wouldn't count on *him* being much help anymore."

Jordan's heart jumped a beat. So now Gilroy was dead. Had he tried to confront Harris after all? The fool, the childish, egotistical . . .

Suddenly Reingold entered. He looked from Harris to Jordan, uncertain, halting.

Jordan smiled thinly. "Another snoop, Dr. Harris— meet Dr. Reingold. Seems the world is just *full* of people who know about the echo vector . . ."

Harris shifted his gaze tentatively to Reingold. "Doctor," he nodded. He removed his pack of cigarettes again, extended them to Art. "Care for a smoke?"

Reingold glanced nervously from Harris's outstretched hand to Jordan, still poised to toss the open microbial container; then he reached out and delicately pulled a cigarette from Harris's pack.

The move confused Jordan. "When did *you* start smoking?"

"Just now," he said softly. "You should, too."

"Yeah, why?"

Harris lit himself a new one on the stub of his old. "Because cigarette smoke clots the blood, doctor, makes platelets clump, you should know that, that's why it's so bad for your coronary arteries . . . but good for Echo—one twenty-one—it clots the capillary leaks caused by the virus. Minimizes the bleeding." He took a big puff, with a big smile.

Jordan's first thought was to laugh, to think that

200

Chessie saved her own life by smoking. His second thought was darker, and directed at Art. "How did you know that?" he shifted gears.

"I . . . just learned it on the computer," Reingold smiled weakly, pulling the floppy disk from his pocket, holding it up like a dead duck.

Jordan's chest twisted as the universe changed shape yet again. "It's you . . ." he whispered, staring at Reingold.

"What's me?" Art's face fell.

Jordan turned, bobbling the double insights of clarity and betrayal. "You're in on it," he marveled. "You were *with* me when I figured this out tonight. You called Harris, told him to remove the evidence. You're the only one who knew . . ."

Reingold looked scared, accusatory. "You're getting completely paranoid."

Harris took a step toward Jordan; Jordan swiveled on him, canister upraised. "Don't move!" He almost dropped it, tremulous with fatigue and tension.

Harris stopped. Jordan glanced at Reingold again. "Public health officer, wow, you were the perfect liaison for something like this; anybody got suspicious, they'd tell *you* their suspicions, and you could keep tabs on 'em. On me . . ."

"Man, *this* is better than *Watergate*." It was Gilroy at the door, shaking his head with a slow, Cheshire grin.

Reingold jumped back at Gilroy's sudden appearance; almost jumped out of his skin. "Who are you?" he demanded. Jordan and Harris shifted slightly to accommodate this new, startling presence.

Gilroy sauntered over to the desk and picked up the receiver off the cradle of the speakerphone that sat there. "I'm the guy's gonna phone *this* story in to the station before it gets any hotter . . ."

Jordan was completely disoriented by Gilroy. He was shocked to see him here, he wanted to tell him about Reingold's complicity, he wanted to stop this phone call, he wanted to make the phone call himself. He wanted to shout.

Gilroy just smiled, push-buttoning the phone. Since the speaker was turned on, though, Jordan could hear the beeps made by the push-buttons, the tone generators; and the tones formed the first seven notes of "Mary Had a Little Lamb." The same number Jordan had called to reach Breen's "next of kin."

Jordan had a sick, plunging feeling in the pit of his belly as they all heard a woman's voice answer.

"Hello?" she said.

"This is Gilroy, zero-seven-one-one-five. I've got the floppy disk—it came home all by itself. Come on over and get it." He appraised the two medics who stood at opposite ends of the room. "You might have to straighten things up a little, too." Then he hung up.

Jordan could only stare, dumbfounded but understanding much more than he wanted to. "Who *are* you?" he rasped.

"I'm the angel with the flaming sword, buddy," Gilroy opened his arms effusively. "But my friends call me Lone Ranger."

"Took your sweet time," said Harris.

"Fuck you, prince, I do my job, and I do it well."

"You're with *them*," whispered Jordan at Gilroy.

"He works for me," Harris acknowledged.

Gilroy crossed Reingold's path, moving angrily toward Harris. "We *both* worked for Breen, if you want to know, but my job is containment, and I do *my* job right."

202

His voice was menacing, directed at Harris . . . but as he passed Reingold, he swung around, pulling from his belt a long, well-used, wire-thin steel skewer. In a single, swift, commando motion, he slipped around behind Reingold and jammed the savvy spike up into the base of the epidemiologist's skull.

The whole action took less than a few seconds, and was over before Jordan could even know what was happening, let alone react. Reingold went rigid, bug-eyed, every extremity extended in decerebrate posturing, and dropped to the floor, dead. Jordan was still just gaping in horror as Gilroy almost nonchalantly walked toward him.

Jordan backed away. "You're the serial killer," he whispered.

Gilroy demurred. "Makes it sound more grandiose than it is."

Jordan shook his head, confused. "But the police composite sketch I saw was of a skinhead black man, he had a broad nose . . ."

"Ain't that the truth of it, though?" Gilroy scolded, "I think every police composite sketch I ever *saw* looks like an ethnic of some kind, and I think it's racist. I think people witness a crime, nine times out of ten they *assume* the perpetrator was black, and that's what their eyes see, and that's what they describe to the police artist."

Harris shook his head, pissed off. "You flaming asshole, you had to do that here?"

"I suppose you were gonna *talk* 'em into submission?"

"You might have subdued them . . ."

"Hey, buddy, you're talkin' to Mr. Security. I'm a *professional*." He took another casual step toward Jordan.

Jordan backed up, raising the canister, but he was

shaking, now. "I'm smart enough to have told someone I came here tonight, you know."

"That's it," Gilroy nodded, "some people just too damn smart for their own good." He smiled sadly. "Like you, buddy."

Jordan stopped, facing Gilroy who stood before the only exit door. "There are others, too," Jordan said, but his words came out dry, his mouth tasted acrid. His muscles tightened, ready to run, or hit.

"You mean Chessie?" Gilroy raised his eyebrows, then shook his head with an expression that Jordan knew well, the expression Jordan used when he had to break the bad news to the family. "Folks in the ER told me her room number just a little while ago," Gilroy explained. "Four-twelve. Then *she* told me you were over here. Helpful little girl. So I thanked her, and gave her some ether, had to conk that nurse, too, before I changed the IV. . . ."

"Changed the IV . . ." Jordan was seething, now, near exploding from fear and fury.

"Yeah, I mixed in that cocaine you found in Dolores's bathroom. Ought to raise old Chessie's pressure more than enough, I expect. Like I said, like froggy said, time's fun when you're having flies."

"You parasite," choked Jordan. Made him think of Abel's tapeworm story—the eggs, the hammer—and beyond reason, he laughed.

"Whatever," Gilroy smiled, advancing.

"No, *you* say 'Where's my cookie?'" Jordan instructed, then reached into his pocket, pulled out his stethoscope, and lobbed it slowly, in a high arc, to Gilroy.

Gilroy's eyes went to the tumbling scope, his hand went up involuntarily to catch it . . . and in that moment, Jordan swung the weighty canister around like a club, pivoting from his shoulders, catching Gilroy upside the head even as the killer saw the blow coming and started to dodge.

The thing had an inertia to it, though, so even a glancing knock threw Gilroy to the floor, tearing off his wig, lacerating his bald scalp, stunning him nearly senseless. His deadly needle went skittering across the tile.

Glass tubes rattled inside the canister, but unaccountably, the lid stayed on. Harris was picking up the phone to throw it at Jordan as Jordan continued his followthrough, swiveling on his feet . . . and let go when Harris came in range. The canister sailed toward Harris, then past him, toward the window.

"No!" shouted Harris, lunging after it. The cylinder crashed through the window as he got his fingers on it, though, and then he tripped, grasping after it, and stumbled through the shattered window in uncontrolled pursuit.

Jordan rushed across the room, leaned out, looked down: Fifteen feet below, Harris lay moaning on the asphalt of the parking lot. Jordan climbed over the sill, held onto the outer ledge, dangled a moment, dropped the last nine or ten feet, and rolled.

He just lay there, feeling for injury. It was raining steadily now, a cold, heavy drizzle. His ankle hurt from the fall, but not too much. He crawled over to Harris.

Harris was semiconscious, breathing raucously, eyes rolling. His right arm was badly broken—took a funny new right angle halfway between his wrist and his elbow—and blood trickled rapidly from his left ear. He lay on top of the canister.

Jordan extracted it from under him, then just rested

there, leaning against Harris's stuporous body, trying to figure what to do. He had to get to Chessie. He couldn't just leave this here, Gilroy might be up and around any minute; he couldn't carry it all those blocks, it was too heavy. The lip was bent, he couldn't get the top on, virus would be leaking out soon, if not already; his ankle was starting to throb. He looked up at the back wall of the building: beside the dumpster, the local gang had spray-painted their colors, their *placa*. Soy Playboy, Puppet, Spider, Loco. XXIII St. Los Machos.

And there in a small pile of garbage against the wall, some beer bottles, a broken car antenna, and the discarded can of spray paint.

Jordan hobbled over to the pile, got the spray can, limped back to Harris as he shook it, took the lid off the echo canister, and sprayed directly into the incubator, holding the button down until the paint was all gone from the spray can, and permeating the viral cultures. Painting the bugs dead.

"Just goofin' on somebody else's *placa*," he mumbled, jammed the lid back on the canister as well as it would fit, and slipped it back under Harris's body. Then he tossed the empty spray can into the dumpster and set off at a frantic pace in the shivering rain.

He had to get to Chessie.

Had to turn off her IV before her blood pressure went high enough to pop her brain. Harris had said the danger level was 150. Okay, there was still time, her systolic pressure was only 100 when he'd left her. But that was before the cocaine.

He had to save her.

After a block his stride regularized somewhat, to a steady, loping jog. His breath was coming in wheezes, but he couldn't afford to collapse before he got to the hospital. A light taste of salt reached his lips; he swept his tongue up to localize it. Upper lip. He brought his hand up, touched the vertical groove beneath his nose, and looked at his fingertips: blood. His nose was bleeding.

He slowed his pace a little more. The last thing he could afford to do at this point was to pump his *own* blood pressure up too high. Blow his little mind.

He crossed the street, dodging a newspaper delivery truck that seemed to swerve to *try* to hit him. Crazy newsdrivers.

It made Jordan realize there was a gray, foggy, post-dawn cast to the sky—the early risers were out, this was the leading edge of the new day. New Year. The old day was finally over. The end was in sight.

He reached the hospital, panting, desperate, soaking wet; and raced in the first door he came to. Stumbling down the white linoleum hallway, he ran into an X-ray technician, caromed off the wall, grunted, found a stairwell, ran up four flights.

He entered the fourth floor wing at the far end of the hall, away from the nursing station. Stumbled from 426 down to 412, pulled the door open, lurched in.

Charlie was unconscious, slumped in his chair by the window. Chessie lay still as death on the bed, the IV flowing wide open into her arm.

Jordan made another inarticulate sound and ran over to the bedside. The digital readout on the blood pressure monitor was ticking higher as he watched: 166 . . . 167 . . . 168 . . .

No.

He clamped off the IV line. He slapped her face lightly a couple times. "Chessie. Wake up . . . please, wake up."

She wasn't waking up.

He had to get her pressure down instantly. He looked around for the bottle of nitroprusside, but it was gone; Gilroy had dumped it somewhere. Wait, he thought, how did doctors get blood pressure lower in the old days, before all these high-tech medicines and machines? Pressure was a function of force times volume. The cocaine was increasing the force, he therefore just needed to decrease the volume. Decrease the volume of blood in her body. Deplete her veins of blood. Phlebotomize her.

He had to bleed her.

Fumbling, he unplugged the IV tubing from her arm, leaving only the short hub in place, extruding from her skin: Blood poured freely from the vein, out of the open IV socket, down her hand, and began puddling on the floor. Bloodletting. Primitive but effective. This was, after all, how Cheremoya had survived—lost so much blood he'd nearly bled to death, but that's what had kept his pressure down, and that's what saved his life.

Then Jordan had another thought—the crash cart. There had to be vials of medication in there that could further bring her pressure down. Not as effectively as nitroprusside, maybe, but in conjunction with the blood loss . . .

He turned to the cart, began opening drawers wildly, rummaging through them, tossing things left and right, he couldn't think straight, couldn't remember where anything was, his head was feeling funny, like it was expanding, and he could feel the blood running from his nose, now, hot and viscous . . .

He found a preloaded needle and syringe labeled Dyazoxide, and clutched it. This would work. He took it over to the bedside, pulled the plastic sheath off the needle, started to stick the needle into the blood-running IV socket, to inject the depressurizing medication; but his hands were shaking too much, he kept missing his mark, he couldn't connect.

"Please don't die," he whispered.

At last he got the needle in place, began pushing down the plunger on the syringe. But Chessie stirred at that moment, and swung her arm around, yanking out the needle before Jordan could inject.

She's alive, he thought, thank God.

Alive and moving—but in terrible pain. She sat half erect, bringing her hands to the sides of her head with a strangled moaning. Jordan approached her but she batted at him, disoriented, belligerent—from the ether or whatever it was that Gilroy had knocked her out with, from the cocaine in her IV, from the early microscopic leakage of blood into her brain. . . .

Jordan grabbed her bloody hand to infuse his medicine, but she pulled away again, wide-eyed now, confused. The pressure monitor clicked another number every second: 172 . . . 173 . . .

"Chessie, it's me," Jordan pleaded. "We've got to get your pressure down, Gilroy spiked your IV, he's the killer. Come on, now, here's the medicine—look—this will help you. *You need this medicine!*"

She cocked her head oddly at him, as if recognizing an old school friend.

"That's it, you know me," he soothed, "it's going to be okay now, it's all right, you're going to be fine, I'm here now . . ."

Tears filled her eyes, she lifted her hands toward him.

"That's it, kiddo, I'll make the pain go away," he kept his voice calm, hypnotic, taking her bloodied arm, bringing it slowly down to the bed. Slowly, she relented, submitting to his care, understanding somehow.

He brought the syringe back to her hand, to the IV hub once more. That's when Gilroy flung himself into the room, crashing into Jordan, thumping him to the bed.

Reflexively Jordan stabbed his needle and syringe at Gilroy, burying the point deep in the side of the murderer's neck. Gilroy recoiled in pain and trained self-defense, swinging his elbow hard against Jordan's temple and knocking him out cold. Jordan crumpled, unconscious, prone across the end of the bed.

Gilroy pulled the needle from his own neck and dropped it on the mattress. No different from any other knife fight—if you wanted to win, you had to get in close enough to get hurt. He felt at the puncture, swelling already and very tender. Wouldn't kill him immediately, though—he could deal with it later.

Chessie continued to stare at him in blank horror as Gilroy methodically leaned over to feel for a pulse in Jordan's neck. He ignored Chessie entirely until she broke her trance and began pummeling him, throwing her fists into his face. He backhanded her hard, hard enough to send her flipping off the bed completely, cracking her head on the floor as she slid into the equipment against the wall, where she, too, lapsed into unconsciousness.

All the monitoring devices, suddenly wrenched from her chest and arm, registered this traumatic disconnection by emitting a drone of long, uninterrupted, high-pitched, continuous beeps.

Charlie, finally aroused from his stupor, began to stretch in his chair. Gilroy calmly walked over, clipped him on the chin, and put him out again. Then he returned to Jordan, felt for a pulse once more. Good pulse. He turned casually to the crash cart, went through a few drawers, finally came up with the tool he wanted: a six-inch-long silver intracardiac needle. A needle ordinarily used to stick far enough into a patient's chest to reach all the way to the heart, to inject life-saving medicines. Gilroy didn't need it to go that far, though. Only as far as the brain.

He ambled back to Jordan, leaned over the bed, pushed Jordan's head way forward, chin touching chest, to expose the nape of his neck.

But Chessie had bled down to a reasonable pressure now; and as if a veil had lifted, the moment was suddenly clear and raw. She saw the madman fiddling over Jordan with his killing needle, trying to remove the plastic sheath; she knew she was no match for him in a fight, there was no contest; but she remembered some of her medical training.

So she silently stood, pushed the On button of the defibrillator, pushed the Charging button, turned the voltage dial all the way up to 400 watt-seconds, the top of the meter. The red light began blinking on and off as the machine's generator lent its own high-pitched whine to the general cacophony of monitors keening. She removed the two metal-faced paddles from their slots and walked unsteadily three steps toward Gilroy, whose back was to her.

Gilroy finally got the needle guard off and was bringing the spike up to Jordan's skull to ram it home when he heard the sound behind him. He started to turn just as Chessie slapped the paddles against his bald, rain-soaked head and pushed the button.

Blue sparks crackled from one paddle to the other, jumping over Gilroy's wet scalp and through his head.

The massive current hurled him back against the wall, crashing to the floor, thrown into continuous grand mal convulsions, his brain fried by the huge jolt.

Chessie dropped the paddles, trembling, weak from pain and hemorrhage. She was passing normal pressure on the way down, now; blood still flowed over her arm.

And Jordan still lay unconscious before her. Dead? She saw the syringe full of Dyazoxide beside him. *You need this medicine!* he'd shouted at her. She remembered that image clearly. To get her pressure down. Maybe he needed it, too.

She wasn't capable of fine control, though. She grabbed the syringe with both hands, plunged its needle to the hilt into Jordan's thigh, through his pants, and injected as much of the stuff as she could push.

Fading, she toppled from the bed to the floor. Several feet away, Gilroy continued having seizures, his body twitching wildly, a bloody foam at his mouth. Weakly, Chessie struggled up and reached for the nurse call-button at the bedside but she slipped on the large pool of her own blood and slid to the foot of the bed.

She pulled herself up by the sheets, moved feebly back to the call-button, grabbed it, started to push it, slipped back down again, and slipped right into Gilroy, who was still convulsing. But she had the button under her thumb, now, and she was pressing it over and over and over in her hand, or was it in her mind? But then nothing was in her mind, only blackness; and then the absence of blackness.

Part III

SYNE

CHAPTER 14

Jordan opened his mind, but not his eyes. Consciousness. He was alive. But where?

Pain was his first awareness. He inventoried it: a throbbing in his left temple, radiating throughout his cranial cavity in cycles of about one per second; a dull ache in his groin, constant, constricting; a stabbing in his side, localized but swelling to agony at the slightest movement.

His second level of awakening was fear: Was he lying, useless on the floor in the corner of room 412, while Gilroy straightened things up before the final blow?

No, not the floor. He was on something softer than that. The bed in 412, perhaps. Chessie's bed.

Was Chessie alive?

He listened for clues. Grunting? Whimpering? Silence? No, none of these. Rather, a low hum from quiet machines, vented air. An occasional click or beep. Hushed voices. A laboratory smell, of alcohol overlaid with bacterial growth. He was in a laboratory, then.

Genenco, it must be. In the hands of the enemy. The designers of experiment, deciding what designs they had on Jordan, how best to dispose of him, what mutant germs would feast on his carcass.

215

Jordan delicately opened one eye, to know the face of death.

It was the intensive care unit.

Jordan opened his other eye. No doubt about it: the Bay Cities Hospital ICU. He tried sitting up, but was arrested halfway by his various hurts. As he lay there, too stressed to move up or down, a nurse came running over to take his pulse. He knew her, her name was Marilyn, she was nice.

"Marilyn . . ."

"You don't have to talk," she assured him. "How you feeling?"

He felt himself all over. "All in one piece." The realization made him weepy.

"Well it's good to hear it from you. Your numbers all look good, too. I'll go call the doctor and tell him you're up."

"Up? Isn't that stretching things a bit?" He glanced left inadvertently, and saw Chessie lying in the next bed. Unconscious. His stomach sank. "Is she. . . ?"

"She's fine," said Marilyn. "Just a little groggy. Good as new in a few days."

His vision began to swim, and he sank back down to a horizontal position. "Wha . . ." he began, but was unconscious again before he finished the word.

Another time when he woke up, he found Detective Burns sitting at his bedside.

"Afternoon," said Burns.

"Is it?" said Jordan.

"So here's what we got," Burns got right to the point. "In one room one morning, room four-twelve, we got a doctor, a nurse, and a patient, all unconscious, and a

216

Channel Eight reporter in convulsions—and I don't mean laughing."

"He's not a Channel Eight reporter . . ." Jordan started to explain.

"Not anymore, he's not—he convulsed for fifteen hours and then died."

"He was CIA . . ."

But Burns wasn't listening, he was talking. "Your doctor told me not to let you talk, so shut up. Where was I? Oh, yeah, so then I get a call from the Feds. Don't get too zealous in pursuit of the serial killer, they say, it won't be a problem anymore. What won't? I ask. The killings, they say—it's all over."

"Gilroy was the serial . . ."

"So I just came to tell you I'm not gonna break my nuts bucking a federal spookathon. I've got other ongoing, full-time cases—and as far as I'm concerned, this one is closed."

"But that's not . . ."

"So good day to you, sir."

Whereupon Burns stood and left.

Once, he dialed the CDC epistaxis hotline. The buttons beeped out "Mary Had a Little Lamb," and the phone rang twice, but then a recorded message came on the line.

"I'm sorry. This number has been disconnected, and there is no new number . . ."

Jordan smiled distantly and hung up.

He called Genenco, asked to speak with Dr. Harris. Dr. Harris was on sabbatical, he was told. Somewhere in Africa; a long trek from Ouagadougou. He was unreachable, really. Would Jordan care to speak with Dr. Dugowson, who had replaced Harris? Yes, Jordan would.

Dr. Dugowson was quite courteous; unfortunately unable to help. Had never heard of Echo-121, Thomas Gilroy, or Dennis Breen. Was unaware Dr. Harris had broken his arm, or suffered any other injury of note. Perhaps when Dr. Harris returned from sabbatical, in two or three years, he could be of more assistance?

Perhaps, said Jordan.

When he called public health and asked to speak with Dr. Reingold, he was transferred to the director of that section, who was rather disturbed to report that Reingold simply hadn't shown up for work one morning and could not, subsequently, be found. This was rather totally unlike Reingold, hence foul play was suspected, but nothing had yet turned up. Would Jordan care to be notified if something did?

Yes, thank you, said Jordan, remembering Gilroy had called his people from the lab that night, told them to come over and "straighten things up," which is when they would have come across Reingold's untidy body.

The director said he would be in touch, but Jordan didn't bother to leave a number.

He hobbled down to the doctors' office in the ER late one night, to go more carefully through the pile of charts on his desk, the medical records of all the epistaxis patients. But the charts were gone. He asked Barb if she'd sent them back to the medical records department; she said no. So he went down to medical records and asked if the charts had come back here; but they said no, the charts were signed out to Jordan in the ER and hadn't been returned, so they were no longer on file.

So the medical records were missing. As far as the hospital knew, those patients had never existed.

Burns showed up again, to see how Jordan was doing. He had a little more follow-up, too. The last serial killer victim had just been discovered—Dolores Reed, stuffed behind her own refrigerator, dead for many days. Manager smelled something funny, went in and discovered the body.

That was it, though, the killings ended with that one. The papers were now calling him the Christmastime killer.

Jordan explained it all to Burns this time—about the echo vector, and Gilroy the killer, how Gilroy had been trying to kill Jordan because Jordan knew too much, how he'd probably killed Dolores because Dolores was infected, or maybe he was just trying to find out from her where Chessie was.

Burns said he'd done some checking on Gilroy, too. He'd hired on as a newsroom assistant and gofer ("That was just his cover," Jordan explained patiently) about a month ago. No recent work records on him before that, but an old past medical history had turned up at a county facility and one of the VA hospitals—psych ward, but that's all he could find out without subpoenaing records, which didn't seem indicated in a closed case.

Jordan smiled. Maybe the serial killer case was closed, but what about an investigation into Gilroy's death?

"Your friend Chessie explained that," Burns raised his finger, acknowledging the point. "She said you and Gilroy showed up in her room. You told the nurse to take a nap, you'd cover for him. Then, while he's asleep, Gilroy starts horsin' around with that defib-whatever machine, pushes the wrong button, and zaps himself. You run to stop him but trip, hit your head, and you're out cold. Then the Lewis girl gets up to help you both, accidentally pulls out her IV, and faints." He held out his hands as if to say that was obviously the way it was. "Sounds open and shut to me. Just like the serial killer case. Solved 'em both the same day."

Jordan just stared at him. "What about the truth?"

"Truth is, doc, if a psychopathic murderer gets paid back in kind by an honest citizen who happened to stumble into a bungled paramilitary operation, who's gonna call the cops?"

Jordan sighed, with mixed feelings. "Not me," he said.

And the truth was, the urgency of the epidemic quickly deflated. Before he was discharged from the hospital, Jordan made a trip down to the ER one morning, to be greeted with cheers and queries from all his pals ("Love your gown," Gloria winked). But while he was down there, he managed to peruse the ER log, only to find that there hadn't been any patients admitted in over a week with diagnoses of epistaxis, conjunctival hemorrhage, or cerebrovascular accident.

So the epidemic had just run its course, as epidemics do; and now it was over.

And unlikely to erupt again soon. Jordan had taken care of that—first, by destroying all the incubating species of Echo-121 and the about-to-be-released Echo-122; second, by having his lawyer, Nathan, file an injunction in federal court calling for Genenco, Inc. to cease and desist development of all echo strains pending environmental impact studies.

Jordan figured that simply by making it a matter of

public record, he would probably mortally dampen the company's—and the government's—interest in the project. So he also told the whole story to his friend, Merle, a newswoman on the *Herald*, and asked her to get involved in a probe. "Probes are my favorite thing," she said. In any case, it would be in the machinery of the courts for years now. Momentum lost, it would sink; and threatened by even the possibility of deeper public inspection—like a vampire exposed to sunlight, or a fastidious virus—it would die.

So it was over.

He spent most of his time, really, with Chessie. She was longer coming around than he was, but he loved just sitting with her, beside her bed, watching her, being with her. Transforming auld lang syne into new. He looked "syne" up in the *O.E.D.*, actually, and discovered it could mean either "since" or "subsequently," which he thought described his relationships to Chessie rather well. Described his own internal clockworks, in fact. What's your syne? he asked himself one morning. Well, it used to be since, but now it's subsequently.

He and Chessie traded their ends of the story to each other, too, over the days. And, of course, they had a lot of mourning to do together.

Dolores, poor Dolores, had been so brave defending Chessie from an abusive husband, only to put herself in the path of someone so deranged as to defy meaning. Chessie cried whenever she thought of her friend, and would cry for weeks to come.

And Reingold. Jordan felt personally responsible for his death, unable to atone. Reingold hadn't wanted to be there. He wanted to be in a classroom, or a library, where he could philosophize, romanticize, dream. But

221

Jordan's pushiness had ended that; had created a universe without Reingold. A bleak and heartless place, made for Jordan's grief.

Yet finally, outrageous as it all was, Jordan decided he could live with it. After all his pointless ranting and whining about—what?—about the injustice of his hollow, stuffed life . . . well, it was yet a life.

And after a day in which he'd seen, spoken to, danced with, flirted with, taunted, decried, denied, railed at, and bargained with death, he'd at last accepted it. And so felt more at ease in his life.

Somehow, then, he was a changed man; yet he wasn't certain how. Certain only that things were different, now. It occurred to him to apologize to Diana for having been such a shit. So he did.

A last note.

Jordan decided to take a couple of months off, go to one of the Greek islands, rent a villa, put it all in perspective. He wanted Chessie to come with him, but after a lot of soul-searching, she decided she really needed to be alone for a while, a good while, and they probably needed to go their separate ways for the time being. Maybe get back together later; maybe not.

In any case, the day Chessie was discharged from the hospital, Jordan took her down to the ER, to say goodbye to the gang. It was lots of best wishes and see you soons, and then, on the way out, Jordan paused by the door, turned around and looked over the scene one more time—his office, the ER log, the acute bed where Breen had died. It seemed almost like a dream now.

"Reminds me of *A Connecticut Yankee in King Arthur's Court*," he said. "You ever read it?"

"I read the 'Classic Comics.'"

"It was just about this regular guy, from Connecticut, he gets hit on the head or something, I don't remember, but he wakes up in Camelot, in King Arthur's court. And he goes through all these harrowing adventures, and falls in love, and almost dies, and there's this big battle with knights getting electrocuted on all this modern technology he cooked up there; but then it all ends up the way it was before he came, no electricity or anything—as if he'd never been there at all. Except he was really the one who got it to that place. And then he went to sleep, and when he woke up he was back in Connecticut again, as if the whole thing had never happened. Except he had a little flower or something from Camelot, so *he* knew it really happened."

"I thought that was from *The Time Machine*."

"And the other thing that made him know that something had really happened was that he was in love now—and that's because of what happened in Camelot, too; it hadn't been true in Connecticut before."

She kissed his cheek. "Okay, I love you, too. So where's my flower?"

He nodded at the emergency room. "It's like we might have imagined the whole thing."

"So what do we do now?" she shrugged.

He put his arm around her. "Take two bourbons and go to bed with a friend, I guess."

At that moment Jill Fergus rounded the corner, almost bumping into them. "Oh, hi!" she said, pleasantly surprised.

"Hi."

"Hi, Jill."

"Glad I got to see you off. When are you leaving?"

"Fly to New York tomorrow, then ship out on Friday."

"Good luck, you could use the rest." Then Jill looked at Chessie. "How are *you* feeling?"

"Much better, thanks."

"Did all your lab work ever come back?"

Chessie looked unsure of the question; but Jordan's eyes lit up, after a five-second computer lag, lit up like an overloaded terminal.

"That's it!" he shouted. "We cultured your nose for virus that night, the night I brought you in here! Jill swabbed your nose and sent it to the microbiology lab, to grow a culture of whatever was in there. So our lab is growing a dish of Echo—one twenty-one right now!" He stared triumphantly at Chessie. "That's the proof!" he whispered furiously. "It's the smoking gun."

"It's the flower from Camelot," she nodded.

The two of them walked quickly to the micro lab in the basement, right next to pathology. There were a dozen technicians standing around, running various complicated machines—blood gas analyzers, incubators, isotope detectors. Russ Hall was standing off to one side, bantering over a microscope with one of the techs. When he saw Jordan he shouted, "By the way, you missed one great New Year's party at my place . . ." But Jordan simply ran past him without a hello, and went straight to Loren, the tech in charge of the bacteriology section.

Jordan was obviously controlling his breathing so as not to pant. "Loren . . ." he modulated his voice.

"Hi, Dr. Marks, what's the matter?"

"Loren, we sent down a viral culture tube from the ER a couple weeks ago on this lady—Francesca Lewis. Any results?"

"I'll check," Loren smiled affably. He walked over to a large logbook and began running his fingers down the columns, going back page by page. He stopped at a name just as Hall was strolling over. "Francesca Lewis," said Loren, "yes, that was a positive growth. An echovirus."

Jordan almost burst, almost laughed out loud. "Can you type it?" he pressed. "Get the exact strain?"

"Gee, no one asked for a typing on the requisition, doctor," Loren apologized, "so we didn't do it."

"But you could do it now, if I put in a new requisition," Jordan smiled.

"No, we tossed the sample, doctor."

Jordan felt the floor tip. "Tossed it," he echoed in monotone.

"Yes, sir, we don't hang on to specimens, as a rule. No room to store the plates even if we wanted to. Yeah, we threw it out." He saw the look of bereavement on Jordan's face, though, and felt bad. "Sorry."

Jordan's face continued to wilt. Hall, standing beside him now, wasn't aware of the nuances, the implications, the stakes. He just knew his friend Jordan was a man given to passions of many kinds. So rather than even try to sort out the dozens of interlocking details that Jordan's stories were inevitably laced with, he merely shrugged good-naturedly and reassured the old scamp. "Jordan, what's the big deal? Just get another specimen. I mean, if you got this one from something that's going around, then *somebody* out there is still bound to be carrying the bug . . ."

Jordan's shoulders sagged in bewilderment. "It's not going around anymore," he said softly. "Not since."

Hall nodded sagely, his point made, if not taken. "Then what's the big deal?" he wondered.

Jordan nodded vaguely. "No big deal," he agreed, and subsequently went to Greece.

Postscript

This is fact:

In multiple germ warfare experiments between 1950 and 1966, the United States Army secretly released a bacterium—*Serratia marcescens*—into the air or water of unknowing civilian populations around the United States, including San Francisco and New York.

One week following the aerosol release of this species of bacterium into the Bay Area winds, an outbreak of disease affecting eleven patients at the Stanford University Hospital was observed; one of these patients died. (This particular strain of serratia seemed resistant to antibiotics.) Prior to this, fewer than a dozen isolated cases of serratia infection had been reported in all previous history. This epidemic was deemed so rare, in fact, that it was written up as an article of interest in the journal, *Archives of Internal Medicine.*

Experiments in other cities coincided with dramatic increases in cases of pneumonia at local hospitals—though the army, defending its role twenty-five years later, continued to deny any causal relationship.

All medical records pertaining to the San Francisco epidemic have subsequently been destroyed.

This is also fact:

Eight years ago, working in a local emergency room, I saw a patient with flu symptoms and a runny nose, slightly blood-tinged.

"I'm Dr. Kahn. What seems to be the problem?" I said.

"Got a dose of my own medicine . . ." he cheerily explained, and proceeded to tell me an interesting story . . .

Incidentally, his insurance was CHAMPUS.

—J.K.
Los Angeles, 1986